NANCY E. POLIN

EVERNIGHT PUBLISHING ®

www.evernightpublishing.com

Copyright© 2017

Nancy E. Polin

Editor: Audrey Bobak

Cover Artist: Jay Aheer

ISBN: 978-1-77339-478-7

ALL RIGHTS RESERVED

NANCY E. POLIN

DEDICATION

To all the usual suspects. You know who you are. At least you should by now. Seriously.
Also a shout out to my Luna-Bear. Who else, but my favorite pup, would curl under the desk and rest her chin on my foot as I write late into the night? Of course, in fairness, if anyone else did do that, it would be creepy.

NANCY E. POLIN

SOUL RECKONING

Nancy E. Polin

Copyright © 2017

Chapter One

Rowan O'Herley gazed through the open window as the driver threaded his way down the busy, narrow streets of New Orleans. Darkness, crowds, and buildings rising two to four stories on either side of the taxi melded to give her a slightly claustrophobic feel. Her cabbie braked countless times when hordes of jubilant people migrated into the road, some staggering, all laughing. Many clutched various forms of alcohol-infused happiness.

"Is it always like this?"

The driver's dark amused eyes scanned her from the rearview mirror and he shrugged. "Sometimes. Sometimes not. It's just N'awlins."

She wasn't sure if the sentiment was some kind of promise or warning. She hadn't set foot in Louisiana since she was a small child, and her memories were flickers, like shadows on a wall. All she knew was that her mother had refused a trip back, stating a less-than-complimentary opinion of New Orleans. The woman was a stickler for propriety.

Despite the fatigue of a long flight, abundant coffee kept her buzzing inside and her gaze darted everywhere at once. Along with the merrymakers, loud music flooded from open doors, the bass searing through her eardrums. Couples disappeared into the shadows of doorways or alleyways, hands stroking and exploring. Men stood outside titty bars, encouraging college-age kids to step inside. *The girls have to be seen to be believed!*

And Rowan had no idea what the hell she was doing there.

She'd entered into a numb state of mourning upon Uncle Jimmy's passing. That numbness stepped up to joust with shock when she got the news she'd been named in his will. Good or bad, her decision had been quick. A bad breakup, twisting with her mother's horror of her daughter owning a tavern, had set events in motion, and here she was.

The stench of garbage and vomit drifted her direction, and holding her breath, she rolled up the window. The driver had warned her the AC wasn't working, so the heat and humidity of a late-summer night beaded sweat on her forehead. Rowan swiped it with the back of her hand before it could trickle in her eyes.

Maybe it had been a bad call.

Kind of late now, don't you think?

"Shit."

"What's that, miss?" The driver's gaze popped up in the rearview mirror and she just shook her head.

"Nothing." *Just my life sliding into the toilet. No big deal. Move along. Nothing to see here.*

"Sorry about the wait. We're not far though."

"Thanks." She was set to meet Margelene Deneuve to discuss Uncle Jimmy's bar within the hour. She wasn't even sure where she was going to spend the night. The lawyer had mentioned the living area upstairs, but her uncle had died up there. She wasn't superstitious, but all the same, Rowan figured she might opt for a hotel and look at everything in the daylight with fresh eyes.

She recalled a big, lumbering man with the sparkle of life and jest in his eyes. His death still struck her as unreal, and something twitched deep inside. A wave of sadness settled over her and she fought the prickling of tears. Emotions were a private thing. The man driving the cab didn't need to see a display that wasn't any of his business. "You said we were almost there?"

"Yup. The Galloping Ghost is a couple 'a blocks down."

"Don't you mean The Galloping Goose?"

His eyes reflected a smile at her. "Just a nickname, miss."

When she frowned, the smile in his eyes expanded to his mouth. Large teeth flashed in an easy grin. "Lots of history here. It's a very spirited city."

Too tired, she didn't pursue the dubious subject of ghosts. It didn't matter. Every place had its share of stories and local superstition. Los Angeles had tons. Hollywood lore was rabid, especially with tourists.

The cab made a right turn, away from light, noise, and most of partiers.

"Ah, here we go." He jerked to the curb of the narrow lane, set the parking brake, and hopped out to get her bags.

Rowan slit a glance through her window, noting the oblong hanging sign of "The Galloping Goose" with its ornate, flowing calligraphy.

Light-blue clapboard siding, with peeling white trim covered the corner building. It rose two stories, traditional French Quarter cast-iron ensnaring the upstairs balcony. The modern touch of glass-block sidelights flanking the heavy wooden double doors allowed minimal light from the bar to seep out into the murky street without giving a clear view inside.

"You been here before?" The driver placed her second suitcase on the curb and quirked a curious brow. "You friend of poor Jimmy?"

Surprised, she turned to look at him. "You knew Jimmy?"

He smiled again, but it quivered in sadness. "Everyone knew Jimmy. Good man. Bad luck."

Puzzled, Rowan tilted her head, looking up at the driver. She supposed having a heart attack was pretty awful luck, but something in the man's sudden anxious tone teased her curiosity. "What did you hear about him?"

The driver blinked and she could have sworn she saw fear pulse over the man's wide face. Unease slid up from her belly to burn in her throat.

He shrugged, but the motion didn't alleviate the obvious tensing of muscles. "Old Jimmy's ticker decided to give out."

He said nothing more as he lugged her bags just inside the bar, nodding in appreciation at the tip she handed him.

The man left a little too quickly, and she frowned after him, perplexed. His attitude bumped up her anxiety, but she pulled in a deep breath and pushed the heavy door inward.

Rowan squinted at the interior of the tavern in the low light. Dark paneling lined the wall to the left, deep-red booths with scarred laminate table tops pressing against it. Directly before her, the bar spread out. A young, dark-haired man leaned against the counter from the business end, talking with some older gents splayed on stools.

Uncle Jimmy's bar. Hers now through a grim twist of events.

The murmur of voices blending with the music of Tom Petty welcomed her in. She half-expected everyone to turn and stare, but no one seemed to pay attention. Due to the enforced smoking ban the previous year, the ubiquitous stench of cigarettes was missing, allowing the aroma of fried food, designer fragrances, wood oil, and pine cleaner to hang in the air in a pungent blend. Even as a non-smoker, she wasn't sure which was worse.

She glanced around, noting with tired amusement the assortment of kitsch lining the walls and shoved into any available corner. Painted masks sneered down at patrons, a stuffed catfish missing one eye swam blindly above two aging pinball machines and a jukebox, nostalgic ads for miracle tonics broke up the dark paneling over the booths, and an alligator head with a troll doll hanging jauntily from its jaws smiled from above the wide selection of liquor behind the counter. Kitty corner to the bar, a small raised stage jutted from a distressed brick wall. A cleared space spread before it, serving as a dance floor, she assumed. She wasn't sure if she should be intrigued or repulsed by whole place. If nothing else, it seemed so Jimmy.

Leaving her cases to the left of the door, she wove her way forward and slid onto a barstool. The bartender stepped away from the laughter of the old men and raised an expectant brow. She blinked in surprise but kept her expression neutral. His face could have been sculpted with an artist's knife in the perfection of another time. A straight nose, smooth, clear brow, the slash of cheekbones, and a full-lipped sensual mouth that should have been soft, but somehow wasn't. Maybe if he smiled, but his expression appeared closer to a glower than anything remotely friendly.

She cleared her throat and spoke to be heard above the din. "I'm here to—"

"Ms. O'Herley?"

Rowan turned to see a middle-age woman rising from one table near the bar. Her shiny, dark hair was pulled back from her face in a low chignon, leaving an honest view of a square face with wide-set eyes and round cheeks. Her makeup was light, but accentuating. Obviously she was choosing not to hide from her age. She strode forward with purpose, a few extra pounds on her tall frame well distributed and lost in confidence.

"It was the combination of bewilderment and mild horror on my face that gave me away, wasn't it?" Rowan accepted the offered hand and gave it a squeeze before releasing it.

The woman laughed, white teeth gleaming in the dim light. "Yeah, that and the suitcases in the corner. I'm Margelene. Margie, if you don't mind. I'm sure you're tired from your trip, so if you'd like, we could just do the bare essentials tonight and take care of the rest in my office in the morning."

"I'd appreciate that." Relief swept through her. Tons of paperwork wasn't something she'd been looking forward to tonight.

One of the oldsters huddling at the other end of the bar turned to stare, before breaking away and scuttling toward them. Permanently bent forward, he still sported broad shoulders and solid arms, but his eyes were lost in the weathered cracks of his face. A wiry mop of salt-and-pepper hair whooshed out from the sides of his head, thinning to a trickle on top. "You must be Jimmy's little niece. He sure talked about you. Smart, pretty, successful. Yeah, yeah, he didn't lie. At least about the pretty part." He wheezed with laughter and shifted to throw a look over his shoulder. "Did he, boys?"

Concurring hoots and catcalls blasted their way and Margie stared at them in admonishment. The hoots drifted away.

Embarrassed, Rowan clenched against the slow warmth creeping up her neck. At least the light was low. She held out a hand to the elderly man before her. "Rowan O'Herley."

The man took her hand, and his smile allowed the shine of brown eyes to peek out from slits within his crinkles. "Henry. Resident fixture since I retired." His eyes lost their sparkle when his face turned somber. "Your uncle was a good man. Good friend. I'm sorry for your loss."

"Thank you."

"We'll get your bags. Make sure they get to the top of the stairs for you."

"Thank you, but I—"

He'd already grabbed one of her cases and a second man, younger by a couple of decades, loped over to grab the other. He shared the same shade of brown eyes and wiry brush of hair, only thicker on top. He tipped his head. "Andy. Nice to meet you, ma chère."

Before Rowan could say another word, her suitcases were heading off without her. She watched them go and sighed.

Margie propelled her forward, a friendly arm looping with hers. "The mute behind the bar here is Luke. Acting manager, bartender, also handyman extraordinaire when in the mood."

Rowan held out a hand and introduced herself again.

The man stared at her outstretched fingers before his deep-blue-eyed gaze found hers and held. A tiny tremor zipped up and down her spine at the intensity of his look and how it bordered on hostile. Her hand disappeared into his in greeting, his touch firm but gentle. "Ms. O'Herley."

"Luke…?"

"Meunier." He pulled his hand from hers but didn't break eye contact. She stared back, feeling a little childish but unwilling to back down. Luke finally looked away to turn and speak to one of the other men huddled against the bar. Something about the Saints. She'd been dismissed for football and pressed her lips together.

Margie tugged her to the side and Rowan managed to ignore the bartender's rudeness in favor of being overwhelmed. The older woman introduced her to hordes of other folks, including Sonny, the cook, a server named Christy, and what was the other one? Taylor? Or was it Tanya? More regulars … Pete, Jace, Bill, Dave, Bea, Layla, um … she couldn't keep everyone straight any longer. She peered around the bar, trying to find and nod at whoever made eye contact, thinking it might be good business, debating about running into the night screaming. Finally, the woman took pity on her vacuous stare. "I'm so sorry. I tend to get carried away. Close-knit folks here. Let's just go ahead and show you upstairs."

The attorney led her past the bar and the small kitchen where Sonny had returned to flip a couple of greasy burgers, and through double doors into a narrow hallway with restrooms, a payphone, a door marked "office", and one simply reading "private." She was propelled to the door at the very end. Pushing through, a staircase suddenly jutted off to the right. Rowan followed her up the protesting steps. "If you stay to the sides, they creak less. What can I say? It's an old building."

Sliding her hand along the bannister, Rowan could envision original wood under years of grime. Genuine interest and curiosity sliced through her haze. "How old is it?"

"Built in 1804."

"Wow. I had no idea."

"Yes, I'm sure it's seen a lot of history. I've been meaning to read up on it, but haven't found the time. Maybe that would be something for you to pursue now that it's your place. Do me a favor and let me know if you find out anything interesting." Margie glanced over her shoulder, mouth smiling, eyes thoughtful. "Here we go."

Margie pulled keys from the slash pocket of her jacket and unlatched top and bottom locks of the one door off the crest of the stairs. As Henry had promised, her bags waited outside. "I had a professional service come in and do some cleaning. Jimmy, bless him, wasn't the best of housekeepers."

Another whoosh of pine-scented cleaner greeted her when she grabbed one suitcase and stepped inside. Beneath it, she caught the telltale aroma of new construction.

At about 550 square feet, the apartment was small, but efficient. The dining room and kitchen combo stood to her left, separated from the living area by a breakfast bar. To her right, French doors led from the main space to what she presumed was the balcony she'd spied from below. She caught a glimpse of the bedroom down the short hallway directly before her.

"Bathroom's off the bedroom." Margie had grabbed Rowan's other bag and deposited it next to the scarred coffee table separating the dusky rose-colored sofa from the TV and stereo rack. "We also took the liberty of stocking some staples in the fridge for you, including coffee. I hope that wasn't too much of an assumption on our part."

"Not at all. Thank you." A smile of pure java-induced gratitude cracked through her fatigue before slipping a little as her gaze continued to roam. "Smells a little like new paint and wood in here."

"Ah, yes. Luke had to do a little bit of work. The French doors are new and there were some marks on the wall that he patched up. I guess he figured a new wall color wouldn't hurt." Margie gazed at the smoky blue walls with a hint of fresh recognition and Rowan wondered when she'd last stepped inside. The woman's tone slid into business a beat later. "We can discuss everything and take care of all the paperwork in the morning, but there is something you should know tonight."

"And what's that?" Rowan's attention wavered to her uncle and a rash of gooseflesh prickled along her arms. He'd passed away in here. She wasn't superstitious, but she was tired enough for her brain to mess with her. Dimly, she debated couch or bed tonight. Maybe the couch. It was closer to the door.

"Your uncle was very specific when it came to Luke."

"I don't understand."

"Jimmy insisted that he always have a job here."

"I guess I can work with that." If nothing else, she'd just have to establish a definite employer-employee relationship. The guy set off her alpha-male radar and she'd already had enough of that crap in her life.

"That's good to hear, because he also lives downstairs."

"There's another apartment?"

"No. He has a space in the storage room, but he does come up here to shower."

Rowan turned to stare, her muddy brain trying to struggle to the surface and clarify the words coming from the lawyer's mouth. "Excuse me?"

"He lives on premises and has for several years. Your uncle stipulated that wasn't to change, unless Luke decided he wanted out, of course."

Opening her mouth, she closed it, and opened it a second time. Seriously? "So, there's a surly bartender living in the storage room?"

"Yes."

"And I can't evict him from said storage room?"

"It wouldn't be easy." She reached out and squeezed Rowan's arm. "I know it's an odd situation."

"That's a word for it."

"Luke is a little abrasive, I know, but he's not a bad man."

Rowan lowered herself onto the arm of the sofa, a frown rippling her brow. "Why would my uncle do that? Or I guess, more to the point, why would this guy even want that? Who would want to live like that?"

"To be honest, I don't really know. I've heard whispers of rumors, but none of the guys really talk." She smiled and twitched her brows.

Rowan read "boys' club" all over the lawyer's expression and fought back a sigh. Perfect. She supposed she shouldn't have been surprised, but it was an additional hurdle she didn't need.

Jimmy always had a big heart. Often, in a derogatory way, Rowan's mother would tell stories about how he'd always bring home strays of all shapes and sizes as a kid. And those 'strays' weren't only limited to dogs and cats. He'd brought home baby birds, a couple of snakes, several toads, a lost ferret, and once, a school friend who was angry that his mom wouldn't buy him a new bike. She wondered what kind of stray Luke Meunier classified as.

"Of course, he may decide it would be a good time to, um, move out and spread his wings or whatever." The man's image did a quick turn in her brain and she shoved it out. Idiot. Logic before hormones.

"Perhaps." Margie's dark eyes caught hers, a hint

of amusement bouncing around that had Rowan frowning. "Anyway, I'll leave you to get settled. Would 11:00 tomorrow morning work for you? I have a couple of appointments earlier. You have the address still? It's only a twenty-minute walk. Perfect way to learn the neighborhood."

Rowan nodded, her mind slipping and sliding.

"Oh, you're going to need these." Margie reached out to deposit a ring of keys in Rowan's hand before giving her a friendly arm squeeze.

"Thanks so much for everything."

"Very welcome." The older woman slid through the door. 'See you in the morning."

After the lawyer disappeared, Rowan continued to sit on the sofa's arm. She glanced around at the apartment, looking but not absorbing.

She shook her head and wrapped her arms around herself against a sudden chill. "What the hell have I done?"

Chapter Two

At one AM, Luke shooed the last regular out and locked up the building. Sonny was in the back cleaning the kitchen, while Taylor and Christy wiped down tables and straightened the dining room.

His mind hadn't stopped its crazy pinwheel all night. He'd known Jimmy had left the Goose to his niece, but from his understanding, she was some kind of actress on the West Coast. If she was juggling a career like that, hell, the last thing he would expect would be for the woman to hop the first flight and move in to the little apartment upstairs.

Maybe it had just been wishful thinking on his part, but he'd hoped the tavern would have been left in his care, or at the very least, Jimmy's beneficiary would have hired a management company. That would have made sense. Especially after what had happened.

Yet here the girl was, ready to be underfoot and pull the owner card.

Then again, it was possible she was unaware of the details.

Luke pressed his lips inward and his jaw tensed.

Her image paraded within the walls of his skull. She was nothing like he'd expected. At all. Jimmy had been a great guy, but with his broad brow, bulbous nose, and thick fish lips, he had hardly been what anyone could construe as good-looking. As a result, Luke had kind of expected Rowan O'Herley to resemble a lawn gnome, but without the little stocking hat or beard. He couldn't have been any more mistaken.

Grabbing both register tills, he turned to shove through the double doors and head toward the cramped business office. Agitation crept under his skin and he couldn't decide if he wanted to take a late-night ride on the bike or blow off steam with some calisthenics. Hell, maybe both.

Or not. Annoyed with himself, he shook his head and clenched his jaw.

Pulling his keys out to unlock the office, he stopped and pivoted when the stairwell door closed.

Rowan O'Herley stepped under the bright halogen lights, her gaze roaming before catching his.

There it was. She and her uncle shared the same odd eyes, a pewter gray with slivers of black floating within. The resemblance between uncle and niece crashed right there though. Jimmy may have sported some sparse strands of ginger, but this girl had hair the color of rich, polished cherry-wood and the smooth, natural cream complexion of near-perfect genetics. The curve of her cheekbones and small, slightly upturned nose complemented the delicate sweep of her jawline and throat. She was breathing evidence the other side of the family must have been dominant. Even the deep shadows hollowing her eyes didn't disguise that kind of beauty. It also guaranteed some long nights for him. Luke tried not to stare, choosing to pretend indifference instead.

He'd really wanted, even needed her to look like a lawn gnome. God, he felt like such an asshole.

"I'd think you'd be sleeping the sleep of the jetlagged."

She shrugged, looking past him before bouncing back. "Same here. Too tired and too wired, I guess. Thought I'd observe closing procedures since I'm up."

"You ever run a business?"

Rowan hesitated before lifting her chin. "I took some business courses when I was in school."

"Business courses." He smirked, turning to let himself into the office. "Not exactly real-world experience."

Her face stilled, but color rose in her cheeks. "Don't worry, I'm a fast learner."

"Hope so. I'd hate to see the Goose take a dive. I've grown quite fond of her." Luke shouldered his way into the small room and dropped into the threadbare desk chair. Logging onto the computer, he brought up the necessary screens before he started counting down the tills, aware the girl had followed, her gaze intent upon his actions.

"Feel free to explain while you go."

He bit back a smile at her dry tone, but verbally noted his steps, keeping his words clipped. The young woman stepped close, leaning over his shoulder to gaze at the computer screen. Despite her long day, a soft scent of orange blossoms lingered near him. Something inside tightened, his lungs suddenly slower to pull in oxygen. He cleared his throat and wished she'd step back.

Her questions were smart, direct, hazing his doubts, but not eradicating them. It was way too early to tell whether she'd be an asset or a detriment to the old place. But it wasn't too early to consider she might be a problem for him.

Initially, he'd guessed her age barely out of her teens, not much more than a child, but he'd now upped his estimate. Life experience coated her like a mist, evident in manner and movement. He wondered what her story consisted of, but he cut off the thought before it could flourish. No. He didn't want to know.

"Oh, my goodness, what are you doing up? You must be exhausted!" Christy peeked into the office, reaching behind her to undo her apron, her expression thick with disapproval. "Pauvre fille!"

"She's a big girl, Christy." Luke didn't look up, continuing his paperwork. From the corner of his eye, he saw Rowan frown in bemusement.

The older woman clucked her tongue and stepped into the office to wrap one arm around Rowan and pull her toward the hallway. "Be quiet, Luke Meunier. The girl's obviously ready to drop."

Glancing up, he caught the expression of utter incredulousness on Rowan's face at Christy's maternal fussing. He dimly wondered what the girl's real mother was like. "I think you're scaring her, Chris."

"C'est bête!"

"It's not silly. Look at her."

"It's fine. Really." Rowan smiled at the other woman, the gesture encompassing her entire face, and Luke took a moment to stare. A yawn followed and she covered it with the back of her hand. "You might be right, though. Maybe I should try to grab a bit of rest. Tomorrow is more than enough time to work on learning the ropes."

"You bet it is." Christy guided the young woman out, chattering at her, asking questions with the relentlessness of a machine gun. A moment later, the metallic slam of the stairwell door echoed through the hallway. Luke presumed the waitress had been successful in her endeavors to shoo Rowan O'Herley back up to the apartment.

Relief settled within, tangling with the buzz of anxiety in a disparate mix. Luke leaned forward, his head dipping into his hands.

Why the hell did Jimmy have to up and croak on them all? He wouldn't be in this position if the old guy was still alive. Luke missed him. He missed long conversations over a couple of beers. Politics, sports, women, gambling, sometimes the past if Luke had had a few too many.

Unbidden, the memory of James Broussard's

body flooded his mind and Luke pressed his fingers to his eyes and rubbed. Fireworks popped at the pressure but did nothing to dissolve the image. The slide of footsteps had him looking up to blink the shooting lights away.

Sonny leaned against the doorjamb to wish him a goodnight, grinned, and raised his bushy brows. "She sure don't look like Jimmy, eh?"

"Fortunately for her." The cook's leering but harmless mug chased death from his head for a moment, and Luke's lips quirked.

The man let out a gusty donkey bray of a laugh, but sobered quickly. "You, uh, think she'll be okay?"

"Why wouldn't she be?" Luke's stomach gave one dull throb as he studied the cook.

He lifted and dropped one thick shoulder, but his grin returned. "'Course she got a big, strong man downstairs if she get scared … or lonely."

"'Night, Sonny."

"Okay, okay. I get gone. The ladies are ready to leave too. I'll walk them out."

"You do that. I'll see you tomorrow."

He heard the murmur of conversation, gossip, no doubt. The girl upstairs would be big news for a long while to come. The heavy slam of the steel back door reverberated through the old building and Luke let out a sigh.

No. Nothing was what he'd ever hoped or expected.

Finishing up, he closed down the computer, stuck the registers and deposit in the safe, locked the office, and strode to the door adjacent to the stairs. Using his key, he let himself in, flipped on the lamp next to the bed, and flopped on the mattress.

Luke lay back against his pillow, staring up at the

unfinished ceiling above him. He had a chest with clothes and toiletries, a borrowed novel, and his guitar propped in the corner of his small space. The rest of the room was devoted to storage, and that was okay with him. Had been for quite a while now. He didn't need much. He'd learned that needing and wanting only led to crippling grief and he had no intention of following that thorny path again.

He thought about the young woman above him and wondered if she'd been able to get to sleep. That wonder evolved into worry as the image of Jimmy's body soaked into his brain for the second time that evening.

No, it would be fine. Whatever the old man had gotten tangled in couldn't possibly affect his niece. Why the hell would it?

Disquiet remained and he softly cursed. He didn't want to get involved. As he pictured the guarded sadness in her eyes, he reminded himself that he didn't want to care. He couldn't afford to.

On a whim, he pulled his wallet from the front of his worn jeans to gaze at the single tattered photo next to his driver's license. He traced the two faces with a reverent finger, looking for some semblance of comfort. Instead of sliding into bittersweet memories, persistent hollowness inside echoed dully.

Luke replaced his wallet and closed his eyes.

Chapter Three

Rowan floated in twilight. Thick humidity pressed to her skin, coating it with a thin film. The water beneath her lapped gently, just as warm as ambient temperature. The shimmer of stars above lay bright against the infinite darkness, and she found herself smiling toward the heavens.

Relaxed, she hovered, not thinking of the past or the future. The mental blankness felt freeing and she wished she could be thought-free more often.

A light breeze licked at her, shoving at the humidity, cooling her overheated skin. Stretching, she tilted her head back, hair spreading across the surface of the water. In the daylight, it would breathe like dark fire, but night subdued the flames into ink.

Her peace ebbed away as images of her family slid behind her eyes. Her mother weeping, her father supporting her with one strong arm. Their actions were uncharacteristic, and confusion fogged her brain. The two of them began to wave, their figures shrinking and blurring in the distance. Even her dream-self recognized the symbolism for what it was: a break in the family dynamic, courtesy of her "bad" choices. Of course, it had been a long while in the making. She'd more or less stopped listening to her mother years ago.

Not that the disappointment lighting the woman's eyes had ceased to hurt.

Isolation stripped away her peace, burning her eyes, stinging her nose. She blinked back persistent tears while a pang of sadness darted deep inside her heart.

Another figure replaced them and Rowan frowned as she squinted toward him, depression dimming. The image pulsed and yawned and became a semblance of human before crystalizing for a moment into the unfamiliar and disappearing the next instant. Her vision was left with emerald eyes hiding within a sketch.

"Rowan…"

The word teased her consciousness, the voice unrecognizable and less than a whisper. It penetrated into her mind with the hiss of a snake, blanketing her thoughts, prickling the base response of panic.

She tried to calm her thoughts and concentrated on easing her rabid breaths. Still unsettled, she gazed back at the stars, seeking comfort in their beauty and vastness, but they were no longer visible. A heavy cloud cover crowded the night sky as the breeze strengthened to a strong gust kicking up around her. It brought waves to white-capped peaks, crumbling her self-control as the sea whipped into violence of an incoming storm. Her heartbeat thudded in her ears and Rowan seized to float and flipped over to swim toward the shore.

She must have drifted farther than she'd anticipated. Land once within easy sight had dissolved into a dense murkiness, and Rowan lost direction. Waves slapping from all angles had her struggling to keep her head above the churning foam, scissoring her legs against the current.

The sound of a man's deep chuckle assaulted her ears the moment a strong, bony hand clamped around her ankle to pull her into the tepid depths. Rowan kicked out, trying to shake the grip, fear rising to terror when she couldn't break free. She flopped on the surface, arms slapping, mouth open to scream, gargling when salt water rushed in to fill her lungs.

****

Rowan jerked from sleep to brilliant morning sunshine slicing into her eyes through the glass panels of French doors. She blinked and squinted around the room in panic, memory blank. Her breathing came in harsh rasps and her heart seemed to pound through her entire body.

Trembling, she sat up to look around, allowing the throw tucked around her to slide to the floor.

That's right. My uncle's bar. New Orleans.

In an unprecedented move, Uncle Jimmy had left this place to her. Rowan still found it unbelievable. It was even more unbelievable that she'd made the choice to actually move to Louisiana.

Christy had shooed her upstairs, prattling on about her need for rest. The woman's careful maternal meddling had been, at once, annoying and endearing. There'd only been concern in her warm brown eyes, so Rowan had let it slide. After all, she'd been right. The day had been exhausting.

Despite the unexpected comfort of the old sofa, Rowan didn't feel rested. She'd collapsed by two, and seven hours of fitful sleep left her hazy and headachy. It also left her uneasy.

Damned dreams.

Too much emotion, too much insanity. Too much … change.

Rowan pressed her hands to her face, rubbing downward before looking around again. Details which avoided her blank eyes last night now came into focus. LPs lined the bottom shelf of the stereo rack, the one visible record from Blue Oyster Cult. Above the TV, two framed lobby cards held a place of seeming honor: Blondie and Supertramp. The bar separating the living room from the kitchen was swept clean with the exception of one statue about eight inches high.

Pushing to legs still a little wobbly, Rowan crossed the small room to inspect the figurine. Picking it up, she ran a thumb over the head. The skeleton crouched in a position of prayer, a cape spread over its shoulders. Etched on the base were the words "San Pascualito."

Frowning, she stared at the crude likeness of bones and the wide, toothy grin. It meant nothing to her and she replaced it.

There were no other personal items in the living area. It could have been a shabby motel room if she didn't know better.

Glancing at the time, she shoved the nightmare behind her and headed for a shower and a change of clothes. Despite her misgivings, there was only one thing she could do. She needed to move forward.

****

Rowan took a long moment to analyze the route to the lawyer's office before shoving her phone in her pocket. The French Quarter was basically a big square, so she didn't figure she'd have too much of a problem. Maybe she'd do some exploring after her appointment to get a feel for the place. The previous night of bedlam and long, dark shadows had succeeded in sparking her disquiet. No doubt it had served as a catalyst for her odd dream. In the light of a new day, she wanted to at least give the place the benefit of the doubt.

Den of iniquity.

Her mother's words pummeled her. She shook her head and rolled her eyes in response. The woman had always been a little over the top.

Locking the apartment door behind her, she grabbed hold of the bannister at the top of the stairs and descended the first step. A cold breeze touched her skin and the strong scent of roses permeated her sinuses. Puzzled, she stopped to glance around. The landing was small and square, essentially only leading to the apartment, but above to her left, a vent rattled, blowing an anemic trickle of cool air.

A moment later, the aroma was gone.

It was too early for the choice fragrance of a customer to somehow recirculate upstairs. Shaking it off, she chalked it off to memory sense. Her paternal grandmother had nurtured roses in her tiny backyard when Rowan was little. She still remembered her clumsy attempts to "help," which consisted of playing in the soil and running with the hose.

Smiling at the image, Rowan trotted down the steps and shoved the door at the base of the stairs outward. When it bounced back, she let out an undignified yelp and stumbled, catching herself before she could land on her ass. A big hand grabbed the edge of the door to keep it from slamming.

Luke stood frowning down at her, eyes deep, contemplative. Almost mocking. Despite the warm day dawning, he wore a long-sleeved t-shirt capping his black jeans. "Problem?"

"No. You just startled me." She kept her tone cool, even as her heart restarted. She allowed a personal pat on the back when her voice didn't tremble.

"Sleep well?" Something in his words had her eyes narrowing. On the surface, they sounded caustic, but his eyes darkened with what might have been concern. It disappeared a moment later and she figured she'd imagined it. It wasn't like the guy had done anything to hide the fact that she was unwelcome.

"Of course. Why wouldn't I?" She jutted her chin out.

"New town. New place." He shrugged a solid shoulder. "I gather Margie mentioned my arrangement."

Rowan stared up at him, at a complete loss.

One brow jerked up. "She didn't tell you?"

"Tell me...?" A second later, Margie's words echoed in her brain. Shared facilities. Biting back a lengthy groan, she nodded. "Oh. She did. Warn me, that is."

"Good."

She swallowed the urge to question him, suspecting he wouldn't answer her anyway. Living within the walls of the tavern was bad enough, but sharing the facilities with her? It felt utterly ridiculous. He didn't seem impaired or anything, so why the hell would he be okay with this kind of arrangement?

"All right then. Don't worry about the key. I have one." He stepped past her, whistling as he took the stairs two at a time, towel and shaving kit under one arm. In his wake, she caught the scent of faint cologne, soap, and warm male. A low tremor heated her skin and she took a half-step back.

Rowan shook herself off but stared after him, noting the grace and power in his fluid movement. Obviously a man who took care of himself. Even more ammo for her bafflement.

With a heavy sigh, she walked toward the front of the bar to let herself out into the brilliant sunshine. She had a lawyer to see.

Chapter Four

It had been all about timing and Marcus Ady could only take that good fortune as a sign from the gods. He seldom voyaged into the city these days, at least not in person, but business sometimes beckoned or certain rare supplies occasionally needed replenishing.

With more than idle curiosity, he'd stopped across the street from Broussard's tavern as the cab rolled to a stop. The woman caught his attention when the driver carried her luggage within, and he found himself wandering over, discreet in his step and gaze.

The building hadn't wanted him there, he could feel the push, unpleasant in its persistence. Marcus clenched his jaw, took a breath, and slipped through the entry anyway. He chose an unobtrusive corner table where he could get a clear view of the room. When the server swept by with a large smile, he ordered a beer on tap that he had no intention of finishing. Trying to ignore the creeping of his skin as the tavern reacted to his presence, he kept an eye on the newcomer.

Young, not even out of her twenties, with dark-red hair and delicate features. Her demeanor held a no-nonsense quality as she was introduced to the staff and some of the bar's patrons, despite the shadows of fatigue soaking into her face. She glanced around, gaze fixing on other customers, smiling, nodding, and finding his and holding for a moment. Those evening-storm-gray eyes left his and moved on. With the exception of those odd eyes, she looked nothing like Broussard.

When the waitress returned with his pint, he smiled at her and nodded in the other woman's direction. "Who's that?"

"Oh. New owner."

"Beautiful girl." The words came out in appreciation and a wave of regret swept through him. It was unfortunate, but there was nothing else to be done. His choices were and would remain narrow if he didn't make a grab for this opportunity. A thread of new resentment sifted through his belly and pooled atop the old anger.

The waitress glanced over in frank assessment. "She is. She's the former owner's niece. He left her the place. Came all the way from California."

"Really? That's going to be quite a change."

"I suppose so. No way she can ever replace Jimmy though."

"Of course not, but sometime fresh blood can invigorate a place."

She leaned a hip against the table and tilted her head. Blonde hair flowed over one shoulder. "I guess. Did you know Jimmy?"

"Here and there." He smiled again. At one time he could charm women, and when she responded with a sudden relaxed smile, he figured he wasn't as rusty as he might think. His deceased wife had always called him "handsome with a thread of dapper." Maybe that had been true at one time, but illness had a way of warping what was or could have been. When he looked in the mirror, the once appealing face had shrunken to skin pressed over bone. It was less a face and more a horror movie mask.

The waitress hadn't seen the ill man sitting before her, though. She'd seen what he'd wanted her to see, which, he would have to say, was a much more appealing package. It had taken a lot of effort on his part. Too much.

At one time he would have considered laying out some breadcrumbs for the blonde girl to follow. All that youth and vivacity would have given him a nice boost, but a connection could not be established. He didn't have the strength.

It had to be Broussard's niece. Blood begets blood.

He didn't stay long that night, just long enough to dispense a little something for the tavern's new owner to start the process. Even if the girl hadn't disappeared as quickly as she had, he still wouldn't have been able to stay. That unpleasant creeping sensation affected every square inch of his skin, propelling him toward the door. Even worse, the protection of the building shoved his lungs closed and constricted his veins. He could barely breathe and his blood pressure rose to crest into an excruciating headache. When he stumbled outside, warm syrupy air of the Louisiana night provided a welcome relief.

Yes, Broussard had turned things around. It didn't manage to save him though. It had been much too late for that. But he had managed to avoid paying his debt.

And now Marcus suffered for his betrayal.

He grit his teeth at the recent memory as he now threw cracked corn mixed with oyster shell down for the chickens behind his home. His land connected with another's on the very northern tip, the rest backed up against the bayou. Braced on stilts, the little house itself had been built with the reality of flooding in mind. Of course, his own protection spells locked it up tight, even as Katrina raged around him. One of his neighbors had floated past on the second day, bloated and staring. Marcus felt nothing, remembering the hissing of "djable!" as they'd passed one another on the narrow road that adjoined their properties. Superstition fueled terror and Marcus found he enjoyed the power it gave him. Besides, the man had been nothing but a waste of flesh. On the rare occasion he laid eyes on the man's wife, she wore blackened eyes or swollen lips as others might boast expensive cosmetics.

One person's devil was not always another's.

Marcus let out a breath and leaned against the wire of the coop. Fatigue was too easy a draw these days, but he now knew there was a way out. Hope fluttered deep in his chest.

What he'd said to Jimmy's waitress was indeed true. Sometimes fresh blood could invigorate. It could even heal. He'd managed to avoid the call of the reaper for decades beyond his given years, and he had no intention of allowing it now.

He let himself out of the enclosure and slowly climbed the steps to the back porch, clutching the railing to pull himself forward. His breathing rasped and his lungs burned. The weakness enfolding him disgusted him, but he reminded himself it was only temporary. Needing to recoup his strength, Marcus wouldn't be able to leave the safety of his home for a bit. At least not physically. His mind still remained sharp, powerful. It was his strongest weapon. But it wouldn't remain so for long. A quick melding of the eyes established the connection with the girl, but he needed time to cement it before he could move forward. Marcus prayed his soul wouldn't break down in the interim.

He shuffled down the hall to the heart of his house to prepare for his afternoon visit.

Chapter Five

Feeling a little indecisive, Rowan stepped into afternoon sun. Her sense of protocol wanted to bring her back to the Goose. She knew she had so damned much to learn and wanted to hit the ground running, but the lawyer had encouraged her to take some time to explore the city. In fact, she'd practically threatened her if she didn't. Being able to tell the Garden District from the Warehouse District from the French Quarter from the surrounding suburbs could only be advantageous as a local business owner. There was no way to really argue with that bit of logic.

Sighing, she slid sunglasses over her eyes and took a moment to get her bearings before turning down Royal Street to head southwest. According to Margie, she could pick up the streetcar at Canal and Carondelet and it would take her on a mini tour of the city.

Taking her time, she paused to peer through storefront windows into art galleries and gift stores, listening to the buzz of conversation and laughter around her. Street performers sang, danced, juggled, spray painted, and impressed with magical feats. Rowan barely sidestepped being yanked into a conjurer's act by flashing an apologetic smile and quickening her pace. The Quarter throbbed with life and energy and she found herself sluicing off the oppression of the night.

Canal spread wide with two lanes running either direction, while the trolley line speared down the middle. Towering palm trees lined the sidewalks, caressing luxury hotels and sidling up against business signage. Rowan slid along with the bustle of foot traffic oozing out from the French Quarter, turned right, and headed up to the next block to cross the street.

She purchased a day pass from the automated ticket seller just as the St. Charles trolley pulled up, ringing its bell. Several people stepped off and she waited patiently for her turn to board.

From nowhere, a chill trickled down her spine, pebbling a cold sweat across her brow and down the center of her chest. Pausing, she pivoted, ignoring riders pushing around her. The heavy sense of being watched soaked into muscle and bone, and her heart rate spiked.

As far as she could tell, no one was paying the least bit of attention to her. People milled around, immersed in their own lives and problems. She heard snatches of conversation relating to appointments, kids, jobs, parties, and politics, nothing concerning the redhead standing frozen beside local transportation.

"You okay, miss?"

Rowan turned toward the voice, finding herself pinned by a dark gaze flitting between empathy and impatience. The trolley operator frowned, lines cutting into her face. "You gettin' on? Where you goin'? You need help?"

Her breath rasped hard in her ears and the woman's words sounded distant. "Um…"

"I got a schedule to keep."

"Sorry," she murmured and climbed on, stopping once to sweep the street again through concentrated vision. Nothing.

The AC blasted above her as she took a bench seat beneath the window. A shudder plowed through her and she braced when the trolley surged forward.

Imagination. She'd never been lacking in that department. It had been honed to a fine point of late. That had to be it. That, and crappy sleep, were a potent combination. She pressed her fingers to her eyelids, aware of the throb of a low headache building.

"Screw this."

She opened her eyes to the wide grins of a couple of teenage boys. One waggled his eyebrows and Rowan stared at him until he dropped his gaze. His friend elbowed him in the ribs and guffawed.

Okay. This was ridiculous. No one was watching her. Hell, no one even knew her here. A tiny bit of caution in any city was wise, but she'd never been paranoid. And she wasn't going to start now.

Lifting her chin and steeling her spine, she shifted to gaze through the window to absorb whatever the sights might be.

So many people going about their business, walking, jogging, biking, or skateboarding, filled her sight to serve as foreground for the shifting views of hotels, businesses, green neighborhoods with stately mature oaks shielding magnificent homes, museums, and a university. Here and there, she caught the shine of past Mardi Gras beads hanging from trees and power lines, and her brows rose at the implication, knowing she would never have the guts to earn them.

Sunlight drifting through the window and the influx of sights and sounds brought about her dormant sense of adventure, and an anticipatory smile twitched the edges of her mouth.

Much better.

She let out a long breath, imagining misgivings and worries flowing out from her. There was no doubt they'd be back to plague her, but for this moment, she wanted to be cheerfully thought-free.

Frequent stops brought a constant influx of people and she watched them almost as much as she gazed through the window. The mom with two tiny children and two reusable grocery bags, the young man with the earbuds and jerking head, the old couple holding hands, the tourists recording everything, including her. Rowan returned her attention to the passing city, and at the rumble of an empty stomach, she made an impulse decision to bail for a bite of late lunch.

Following a migration, she chose a restaurant at random and sat on the enclosed patio to watch foot traffic. Deciding to skip dinner that night, she ordered a plate of brisket and parmesan fries with an inward promise of heavy calisthenics. She would normally run, but wouldn't until she was comfortable enough in her new surroundings.

Indulging in a glass of Cabernet, Rowan's thoughts began to drift. When she arrived back at the tavern, she planned on sitting down and scrutinizing Jimmy's budget to see what kind of wiggle room she might have. Perhaps she'd be able to spiff up the place a little, but figured she'd have to be careful not to scare off the regulars. The corner stage lent itself to live music at one time and she wondered if that was something her uncle had supplied or if it was an avenue neglected. His books would tell her, or she could always ask Luke.

The thought of him brought a frown. She'd called earlier to touch base, letting him know she'd be out the rest of the afternoon and his dry response had been something to the effect that she should take her time, the place wouldn't need her anytime soon. If she could have shoved a fist through the phone to sock that handsome face, she would have enthusiastically done so.

It didn't matter. She'd make this whole situation work no matter what. She had no plans whatsoever to go home with a bowed head, as much as her mother might expect or even hope. After all, O'Herleys were doctors, lawyers, shipping magnets, and business VPs, not actors and certainly not bar owners.

Tension marched into her shoulders, and Rowan

did a slow roll to keep them from knotting with pain. She took her mother's disapproving image and shoved it away, very aware it wouldn't go far.

When her server swung by with her order, her stomach snarled in anticipation. Coffee had been a necessary starter that morning, but solid food had eluded her a little too long. With more than a little gusto, she dug in, rolling her eyes in food ecstasy. If she wasn't careful, New Orleans would make her fat before she could blink.

As she ate, her mind picked at problems and plans, careful to omit the Luke factor. As long as she could remember, she'd treated her issues like tightened knots, picking and working until she could straighten them out.

"What's a pretty lady like you doing eating all by her lonesome?"

At the smooth voice, Rowan snapped out of her musings and looked up at the man standing beside her table. He gazed down at her, green eyes popping against mocha skin that crinkled in the corners. Something about him yanked a familiar cord in her brain and she frowned. "Just enjoying the afternoon."

"Ah, such a beautiful one it is. Tourist or resident?"

"Both, I suppose." Rowan sipped at her wine, scrambling to identify him, but nothing came to mind. With reluctance, she tried to let it go.

He chuckled. "On the cusp between one and another. Wonderful place to be. Everything is shiny and new. It all gets old much too quickly." The man slid into the chair across from her, his move quick and graceful. He folded his long slender hands together and rested them against the white of the tablecloth.

A tingle reverberated at the base of her skull. "Is

there something I can do for you, Mr....?"

"Oh, no. I'm doing beautifully, but I had a question for you."

Rowan glanced around her. No one paid attention to the odd man hanging about her table, but then again, why would they? "Well, I suppose you can ask, but the answer will most likely be 'no.' No offense."

"What does family mean to you?" He ignored her comment and tilted his head, the gesture somehow knowing.

"Pardon me?"

"Oh, you heard me." He leaned forward, eyes meeting hers. His voice lowered and any semblance of good humor leached away. "Family is very important, c'est vrai?"

"Who are you?"

"Do I seem familiar?"

She stared into his eyes, felt an odd sliding sensation, and pulled her gaze away. A prickle of sweat itched along her hairline.

He shrugged one narrow shoulder, the casualness of the gesture not melding with the steel in his eyes. "You could call me a family friend, ma petite."

Rowan's heart pounded in her throat, the man's presence sending off electrical charges of alarm. Her reaction confused her, but she swallowed her sudden fear and allowed a wave of anger to take its place. She put down her wine, proud when her words bit instead of trembled. "Look, I don't know who the hell you are, but I think maybe it's time you leave."

"Does family mean honor?"

"What?"

He leaned back, his mouth smiling, his eyes not. "I think it's important to meet your obligations, not run from them, oui?"

Rowan stared back and narrowed her eyes. Her heart still thundered but temper won at the ambiguous threat. Breaking the visual lock, she gestured to the server as he passed. Stopping before her, the young man's face queued into polite and attentive. "Yes, miss? Would you like more wine? Or is dessert on your mind? We have an amazing chess pie."

"No, I'm good, but this guy—"

"Miss? I'm sorry?"

She looked across the table to find the green-eyed man gone.

"Miss?"

"Um…" Bewildered, she glanced around, expecting to see the man walking briskly down the sidewalk parallel to the restaurant, but didn't see him. She peered past her server through the entry and into the main hub of the restaurant. He must have gone in there. The inside was dim, patrons indistinct compared to those sitting outside within the sharpness of the afternoon sun. "Um… I think I'm ready for the check, please."

The server pulled his brows together in a frown. "Are you okay, miss?"

Was she okay? The man had vanished. No, that was ridiculous. He had to have gone inside. Either way, she wanted to leave. "I'm fine, thank you."

He nodded slowly, seemingly unconvinced, and she figured she must look as shaky as she felt. "I'll prepare the bill for you and I'll play cashier for you when you're ready. No rush."

Rowan thanked him again as he walked off to grab the check for her half-eaten, now unwanted lunch.

****

Luke glanced down at his watch before he turned to draw a beer on tap for the tired man in the rumpled suit slumped at the bar.

41

The woman had been gone for hours and he wasn't sure if that was a good thing any longer. When she'd called, he'd felt peevish, snappy, and had done nothing to hide it. Her tone indicated animosity was not just on his end, but that could have been a reflection on him, too. He didn't think what he felt was guilt, at least not exactly, but a newcomer wandering the city on her own could be cause for concern, no matter who it was.

Liar.

Sighing heavily, Luke swiped the bar with his towel. He'd been trying not to think about Rowan O'Herley all day and had almost succeeded when she'd called and thrown him off balance. It irritated him all the more when he realized he was, in fact, worried about her.

She didn't need to ever know it though. She might get the wrong idea.

"Bon après-midi, Lukas." Henry slid onto a stool and grinned hard enough to split his walnut face in half.

"Almost evening, Henry."

The old man cast a frown. "Don't hurry things along. Days go by fast enough." He made a drama of looking around, the frown replaced by a smirk. "Where your new boss?"

"Out." Her face pressed into his brain and he remembered the fragrance of orange blossoms. Luke shook his head to dispel the image. "Where are your boys?"

"Ah, they be around soon." Henry narrowed his already narrow eyes, the glint of brown peeking though. A smile played around his mouth. "You run her out already, or did this old place do it?"

"She's out getting her bearings." Luke delivered the man's light beer without being asked, knowing it would soon lead to something with a little more punch.

Henry pursed his lips and took a sip, swiping suds

away with his tongue. "You think that's a good idea? Little girl wandering around N'awlins on her own?"

"She's a grown woman. If she's from L.A., chances are she knows how to handle herself or at least has a tiny bit of common sense. Maybe." Hopefully.

Shrugging, Henry looked unconvinced. Luke could tell he disapproved, but the woman wasn't his problem, or his responsibility.

Both looked up and over when a sliver of sunlight cut between the door and jam of the front entrance. The small figure pushed in and Luke caught the glint of auburn in her hair before the low light of the bar stubbed it out. "See. Safe and sound."

Henry grunted.

"Hey, boss. Glad to see you didn't get yourself lost." He was careful to keep his tone a little sharp, unnerved to realize his heart beat a little faster.

Rowan approached them, greeting the few early-bird customers, glaring at Luke with those smoky eyes simmering.

"How you enjoy our city?" Henry smiled at her instead. "Love at first sight or she gonna grow on you?"

"I had fun." Her gaze latched onto the old man as Luke studied her, weighing how she appeared that morning against her appearance now. A little uneasy, maybe? Impossible to say at this point. He didn't know her.

And he didn't want to know her. His inner voice snapped at him, cool and collected. Interest could lead to caring and caring was the last thing he ever wanted to do again. It was better to avoid the possibility altogether.

"Definitely merits more exploration, but for now, there's a few things I need to see to. You enjoy your drink, Henry." She swiveled to weed her way through tables and head for the back hallway.

Luke watched her exit, noting the grace of her step and how her hair swayed against her shoulders. It was a little tousled, slightly curling up at the ends, no doubt from late summer humidity. Blinking with annoyance at himself, he pulled his gaze away only to look into Henry's face.

A hint of amusement lit the man's eyes and Luke concentrated to keep his expression blank. He raised one eyebrow. "What?"

"That girl look peaked to you?" Henry's smile bled into a frown and he shifted on his stool.

"Probably just a hazard of having red hair."

"Aren't you the wise one?" The old man shook his head. "Always playing everything down."

"Hazard of being a bartender."

"Gonna cuff you one, boy." A laugh erupted deep from within, shifting into a snort. Shaking his head in amazement, he jabbed a finger toward Luke. "My own boy that cynical, I'd cuff him one."

Chapter Six

Rowan didn't sleep.

After an hour of shifting, turning, and sighing, she got up to fix a cup of tea. Her mind wouldn't settle, stuck between the tense excitement of a new situation and the weirdness haunting her since she'd arrived in New Orleans.

The man in the restaurant had left her disturbed, agitated, but worse, she couldn't seem to remember what he even looked like now. It was as if he'd been a figment of a dream or more likely, a nightmare, sliding between her fingers as she'd awakened. And now the more she thought about it, the more she wondered if that hadn't been the case.

The kettle whistled and she steeped her tea bag for several minutes before adding a little honey and a splash of milk. She hoped it would relax her enough so she could grab at least a few hours of solid sleep.

Sipping the hot drink, Rowan felt a little more grounded, steady. This was reality, sitting here in the little apartment. The weirdness had to be a result of change and patchy sleep. Nothing more. Taking another sip, she contemplated plans for the tavern, doing her best to fill her mind with future possibilities and push back any semblance of nightmares.

Tomorrow she was meeting with an inspector, and depending on what she learned, she had already started to research local contractors. Even if the place was up to code, she still had a few changes in mind. They wouldn't be huge, more of a polishing than anything else, but The Galloping Goose would be all the better for it. At least that was the hope.

The sound of breaking glass downstairs made her

jump, spilling her tea. She hissed at the hot liquid against her skin, but forgot about it the next instant.

Rising to her feet, she stared at the door leading out onto the landing, for the briefest moment wondering if she imagined it.

A second crash had her reaching for her cell phone, staring at it in dismay.

Dead.

Hadn't she recently charged it? She could have sworn she had.

The house phone was downstairs. It didn't seem like Jimmy had ever bothered to put an extension or private line in the apartment. Rowan made a hasty mental note to remedy that first thing in the morning.

She hurried into the bedroom, removing the large flashlight from the bottom drawer of the dresser. The thing held about 157 batteries and had the heft of a baseball bat. Her father had gifted it to her before she'd headed east, citing dual purpose. At the time she'd thought he was crazy. Now she wasn't so sure.

The wimp in her jabbered about staying upstairs and barring the door, but the pigheaded side promised hell to pay. This was her place now and no one was going to screw it up for her.

She considered turning on the flashlight but didn't want to expose herself. Holding it tight enough to cramp her fingers, she crossed to the door, throwing back all three locks, and stepped out onto the landing. She waited, listening, wincing when another window exploded.

Pulling in a breath, Rowan descended the stairs, careful to stick to the edges to avoid the inevitable loud creaks from the middle. Darkness wasn't complete, but it was close. Using one hand to glide over the bannister, she clutched the flashlight with the other, fingers already complaining.

Listening at the door for footsteps, she judged her distance to the phone in the office. Not far, just the second door on the left, right after—

Luke. Where the hell was he? There's no way he could sleep through that racket. But then again, maybe he could. Her ex-fiancé could sleep through the apocalypse.

Heart racing to the tune of a hummingbird's, she pushed open the stairwell door, pausing for a moment to see if she could make out light from another flashlight. When she saw nothing, she crept forward, clutching the Maglite like a club. There were only a few more steps to the office, phone, and 911.

Movement to her right had her swinging around as the hall lights flashed on to blind her.

"Whoa, whoa, whoa!" Luke caught the end of the flashlight in his hand before she could club him. "What the hell are you doing?"

"What the hell are you doing?" Rowan hissed back, panic and anger congealing in a nauseating mess in the pit of her belly. "Didn't you hear that?"

He stood before her in a long-sleeved crewneck and sweats, gazing at her, brow furrowing. "What are you talking about?"

"Someone's breaking in, you idiot. Didn't you hear the glass?" Blinking, she darted glances around her and beyond him.

The ghost of a smile pulled at his lips. "No one's breaking in, ma chère."

"I know what I heard." She stepped around him toward the office door, but he caught her by the arm with a brief shake of his head. Rowan pulled free and stumbled back a step. "Are you crazy?"

He pulled in a deep breath and let it out in a slow leak. "Go check if you'd like. There won't be any broken glass."

Narrowing her eyes at him, she hefted the flashlight back into a batting position and crept up the hallway. It occurred to her she was wearing the same long t-shirt she'd slept in, and when she glanced back at Luke, his gaze was, sure enough, affixed to her legs. She bared her teeth and he raised a brow.

Dismissing the "rampant chicken asshole," she pushed through the double doors, expecting to see the block glass flanking the front entry shattered.

Nothing.

No, that couldn't be right. The sound she heard was higher, like thin glass breaking.

It had to be the small windows off the kitchen.

Rowan backtracked past the bar and turned left into the small kitchen. She stepped carefully, unwilling to shred her bare feet on shattered glass but still prepared to concuss a prowler.

Not only were the two windows intact, but she'd forgotten how long and narrow they were, maybe large enough to admit a kid or very determined squirrel, but not the average adult.

Confused, she let the flashlight swing down next to her leg.

Luke stepped up beside her and she briefly considered braining him with the Maglite, but knew she was too tired for bloodshed. Even his.

"There are more things in Heaven and Earth, Horatio, than are dreamt of in your philosophy."

Rowan narrowed her eyes. "Is there a reason you're quoting Shakespeare at me?"

"Look, I'm not sure how open-minded you are, but you're going to hear, see, and smell lots of oddness in this old building."

Rowan turned to look up into his face, expecting

a smirk, but not finding one. "What? You're saying this place is haunted or something?"

When he just looked at her, she chuckled. "Are you kidding me?"

"A lot of history here. Leaves a mark."

She thought about what the cabbie had said that very first night. Dismissed it. But words Luke said boomeranged back into her head and a niggling doubt crept from the base of her brain. "Smell?"

"Occasionally. At the top of the stairs, sometimes you get a waft of roses. She seems benign. Well, to be honest, I think the majority here are. Jimmy dubbed that one 'Mavis.' The glass breaker is 'Robert.' He seems most active when there's someone new around. Seems to agitate him. Or maybe it's his odd way of welcoming you. The last time he acted up was just after we hired Taylor."

Rowan stared at him, her brain trying to interpret and then reinterpret what he'd told her, but failing. This was nuts. She nibbled on her lower lip, noticing when he followed the motion, forgetting it the next instant. "So, Uncle Jimmy named his ghosts."

"He was peculiar that way."

"This is peculiar. You're peculiar. I'm going back to bed. Hopefully this is all some figment of a whacked-out dream."

"Say 'hi' to Mavis on the way up."

She shot him a glare, slitting her eyes when his mouth twisted into a quick smirk.

Chapter Seven

She hadn't set foot in any of New Orleans's historic cemeteries since her arrival, but she stepped through this one as if she'd grown up playing hide-and-seek among this city of the dead. Tall mausoleums topped with crucifixes or somber angels blocked light sifting from the half-moon above, while stone benches and open vases awaited quiet reflection and flowers from the living. Magnolia trees spread their branches, offering shade during the day and crooked shadows in the dead of the night.

Rowan walked softly, careful not to crunch dead leaves under her tennis shoes or trip over the uneven pavement. Terror brought a metallic taste to her mouth and tremors that threatened to bring her to her knees. There was no way to know if she'd even hear what stalked her. The thundering of her heart and the ragged breath in her ears overwhelmed and isolated her.

She took a long moment to rein in her panic before slipping down the narrow space between two concrete graves, looking over her shoulder, but trying to see before her as well. Extreme vigilance would soon leave her exhausted and helpless. She couldn't allow that to happen.

The slide of a footstep against loose gravel reached her, but the sound echoed and she couldn't make out a direction. Stilling, she held her breath and waited.

Again. Closer.

Fight or flight, her body held in indecision and she worried she'd taken the choice behind door number three: freeze.

No, no, no. That choice would be the one to get her killed. If she fought, maybe, just maybe, she'd at least hurt them, leave evidence under her nails. Something, anything.

A heavy sigh whooshed into the air a bare few feet from where she hid.

Her freeze broke and she shoved her way out from between crypts, tripped in a thick tuft of grass, and sprawled forward. Recovering, she got her feet beneath her. Flight was her best choice. She was fast, her wind exemplary. She could beat this.

"Rowan..."

The sigh breathed her name and she pushed harder toward the perimeter gate. From there, she'd hit the street, her mind foolishly convincing her of safety beyond the cemetery.

She wove through tombs, innate sense guiding her. When the locked gate loomed, she bit back a cry but didn't reduce her manic pace. Despite the wicked spires at the top, she decided in mid-flight to hurdle herself forward and try to scramble over the top. It would be better than facing the vile presence pushing at her back.

When powerful claws dug into her shoulders, her screams scorched her throat and tore through the night.

****

"Hey! Hey!"

Rowan scrambled backward and would have tipped back in the chair if the office had been larger. It thudded against the wall and she looked around, wild in her panic.

Midnight-blue eyes stared down at her, Luke's expression inscrutable around them. It took her a moment to realize his hand was clamped down on her shoulder, large and warm. His words were cold water against the gentleness of his touch and she blinked hard up at him in confusion.

"You fell asleep. Good thing we're closed,

otherwise that scream would have scared all the customers out."

Words wouldn't come for several seconds as she listened to her pulse rage in her ears. Her heart had become rabid as it thrashed itself against her ribs, and breath burned her lungs as she fought to catch it.

Luke crouched before her so they were eye to eye and his voice gentled. "Rowan?"

"I'm fine."

He pulled his hand off her shoulder quickly, straightened, and stepped back as if the contact stung. Its warmth was replaced by a sudden chill and a shudder ran though her. She curled forward and ran her palms across her face to hide it. "What time is it?"

"A bit after 1:00."

Rowan pulled in a quivering breath. She'd been sitting at Jimmy's computer, scanning business files, and the next second she was in the cemetery. Jesus. "I just closed my eyes for a second."

"It happens. Maybe it's time to go upstairs and shut them a little longer. I have books to do."

She did a quick scrub of her face and glared up at him. Irritation forced out any tendrils of lingering fear from the nightmare. "Are you always such a dick?"

"Usually. Depends what day of the week it is."

Sonny appeared behind him, big eyes seeking and finding hers. "You okay, miss?"

Now embarrassed, she nodded. Her knees felt like gel when she climbed to her feet, and she held onto the desk for an extra moment as an excuse while she closed her computer screens. She also didn't want Luke to see her momentary weakness. He'd already seen too much. "I'm fine. Heading to bed now."

Legs stronger, she pushed past both men, only to run into the two servers in the hallway. Taylor, a twenty-something girl with blonde hair pulled back in a ponytail, stared, while Christy, older by a good couple of decades, blinked up at Rowan from her top height of five-foot even. "You okay, darling? That was quite a shriek."

Rowan took a breath, feeling stupid. "Fine. Just a dream."

"Hell of a dream."

The warmth of her face had her nodding and turning toward the stairs. Her fair skin flushed much too easily. "Thank you for your concern, but I'm okay. Really. You all have a good night."

****

Sonny watched the young woman disappear through the door leading to the stairwell. "Maybe that girl needs a little protection."

"From bad dreams?" Luke dropped into the office chair, still warm from Rowan. His insides trembled from the woman's scream, but the rest of the staff didn't need to know.

"A little gris-gris never hurt anyone. Maybe this place is getting to her."

"I sure wouldn't want to stay here overnight," Taylor pointed out, and Christy hummed in agreement.

Fixing his gaze intently on all of them, Luke raised his brows. "There's nothing here that would hurt her. For God's sake, she had a nightmare."

In the almost three years he'd been living at the tavern, he'd never felt threatened by any of its inhabitants. He'd been truthful with Rowan the night Robert had performed his odd display of welcome. The ghosts in the tavern were benign, as far as he was concerned. The memory of that night brought an image of her in a sleep shirt, flashing a lot of leg and hefting a flashlight bigger than she was. He bit back a smile.

"What about Jimmy?"

The weight of a stone fell into his gut. He hadn't discussed the circumstances of Jimmy's death with any of them before. "What about him?"

Sonny frowned, his gaze darting around the office, unable to fix on Luke. He shot a glance over his shoulder as if to confirm that Rowan O'Herley had indeed gone upstairs. "Well, you know…"

Luke stared at Sonny and waited.

"I know you feel safe here, but I dunno … what if something here doesn't like her? Like it didn't like Jimmy?"

He supposed Sonny's assumption was a fair one. He'd heard the rumors, as did practically the rest of the whole damned city, but Luke was the one who saw the body and everything in his gut screamed it was something beyond The Goose. "It wasn't the bar. I think Jimmy might have gotten himself into … something else. He just didn't tell me about it."

That knowledge burned him. He might have been able to help, but he'd been forced to watch the old man pull away from everyone and everything for months before his death. And Jimmy never said a damned thing. Luke didn't know if he'd been trying to protect him or perhaps was too terrified to let him in.

"How do you know Ms. O'Herley isn't being affected by … whatever … Jimmy was involved in? It's not normal for a girl that age to be sporting that kind of eye baggage. Her sleep must be crap." Christy crossed her arms over her chest, her expression stern. Luke had a feeling her two young kids shriveled under that look.

"Look, I'm here and I'm not going anywhere. I'll keep an eye on her." The words stumbled out and his heart turned leaden. He would watch out for her, but he wouldn't be able to help himself. So much for not getting involved.

"I thought you didn't like her." Taylor peeped over Christy's shoulder, reddening when Luke stared at her.

He shook his head and waved an impatient hand. "Go home, everyone."

Chapter Eight

Balance.

It was too easy to push too hard, too fast in his zeal. Not keeping balanced could prove dangerous for both of them.

He'd forced himself to pull back to concentrate on building himself up nutritionally and spiritually. Not an easy bridge to erect. His energy continued to wan, a slow leak without end unless he could rectify things, but if he moved too fast, he could lose the girl to a mental break. She'd still be useful but nowhere near to the extent of a healthy mind and body.

Still fatigued, frustration clawed at him, but control was tantamount. He'd only day-walked to the girl once, relegating most of his communication to the dream world. Subconscious prodding was important, but experience dictated the necessity to insinuate himself into her conscious mind as well. And that took much more strength. The constant drain worried him, but by comparison, today was a better day. His time was limited so he would need to take advantage.

The man rose from his cot, choosing hydration and protein, not paying attention to taste or texture. On a cognitive level, he knew his body needed fuel, but he also knew he now ran on a different kind of raw energy. Survival. There was nothing left otherwise.

If he contemplated too much, he'd feel sorry for the girl. She was only a pawn after all, but vengeance sought blood. He found it much more palatable to think of her as a tool. James Broussard had run scared and tried to call it all off, which had been unacceptable. Ady never anticipated the old man's betrayal, and that knowledge enraged him. He should have seen it coming, but the path had turned murky, perhaps a taste of reprimand from the gods for his ego. Marcus had paid penance for his limited vision and Jimmy had slipped into a very unpleasant death. It had taken months of torment and Ady still had not been able to collect the debt. Marcus shook his head at the memory. Stupid, stupid man. If Broussard had known his niece would pay for his betrayal, would that have changed the outcome? Ady couldn't say. Some men had more honor than others.

At the time, it didn't occur to him that the tavern held protection. Broussard's soul had been lost to him because of an old spell. Age didn't make it any less potent. Annoyed, he still wondered about the origins. It could have been purposeful, but then again it could have been the result of a curse that bounced back. Marcus hadn't personally heard of such an event, but knew it was possible. Over the years, he'd learned never to underestimate the gods or those who communicated with them.

Not that it mattered now. Ady acquiesced to facts. Yes, Broussard had managed to elude him. The girl, however, would not.

It was time to reach out once again.

On shaky legs, he stepped into the back room, careful to avoid the lines of the intricate diagram he'd constructed. Against the far wall, a bookshelf filled with jars of standard ingredients, plus many taboo, met the eyes. Every single one had had its use. Some white. Some black.

Removing two jars from the top shelf, he ingested a pinch from the first before returning it to its home. He left the other within reach as he lit candles to join the points of the diagram on the floor. Holding the second jar with a shaking hand, he positioned himself in the center of the drawing, crossed his legs, and let out his breath, controlled and steady. Dipping his fingers into the liquid, he painted symbols upon his naked skin, his motions robotic, trancelike. The murmurs rose from him. Sometimes he was aware when they did, sometimes not. The tongue would not be in a language discernible to any local. Afterward, he would have little memory of it. But he would remember the result.

As he slipped under, Marcus Ady smiled even as his eyes glazed.

Chapter Nine

Luke needed to ride.

He'd been balancing his obligatory watch over Rowan with his aversion to getting too close for too damned long, and the effort left him tense, wired, and ready to snap.

As far as he could tell, nothing more had plagued her in the last few weeks and he could admit he was happy for it. He didn't need the extra worry. On the other hand, this now well-rested, gorgeous woman was always under foot with a flurry of ideas and activities to improve the Goose. Luke could barely move without bumping into her in one capacity or another.

In frustration, he'd made the short hike to storage and now opened up the muscular Fat Boy, heading east.

Last year he'd paid cash for the bike, much to the shock of the salesperson. A rare indulgence he didn't regret. Especially during times like this.

There was no specific place he had in mind, but the sheer act of speed pushing his hair back and throwing his thoughts to the wind brought him into a state of peace as close to contentment as he could ever get.

Early-morning sun barely dusted the horizon, which meant little to no traffic. Between Louisiana and Mississippi, everything was wide open. It also meant his chances of earning a speeding ticket were also wide open. But didn't bother him. It would be worth it.

Thick foliage pressed in from both sides of the highway and he could imagine everything lurking within. Gators that wouldn't be going into hibernation quite yet, black bears, raccoons, coyotes, and who knew what else. Maybe even the Rougarou roamed to keep Cajun kids in line. Hell, he'd been one of them. Whenever he'd acted up, grand-mère threatened him with the legend. It worked up until he was about seven. After that, he'd tried to be good out of respect. Failed miserably at times, but still tried. She'd always given him points for that.

He pushed the bike a little faster, thinking how she would have kicked his ass for not wearing a helmet, and allowed a closed mouth smile around the image to avoid bugs between his teeth.

It fell away the moment his mind shifted and he let out an oath the wind blew right back at him. He hadn't wanted to think about Rowan O'Herley, but there she was, once more, hanging out on his periphery, taunting him.

Anger flared inside, any enjoyment of the impulsive ride shriveling into nothing.

Luke didn't want to picture her. He didn't want to think about the glow of flawless skin, the tumble of hair the color of burnished mahogany, and how those soft gray eyes would sharpen into flint when they were cast his way.

He certainly didn't want to imagine pressing her up against the closest wall to discover how that rosebud mouth tasted or what it would be like to explore the satin of her flesh with his tongue and lips.

There was no way in the world he could put himself through that kind of anguish again. The more intense the love, the harder the fall. It was a lesson he didn't dare challenge a second time. Losing everything once had been enough.

So far, she was only a beautiful woman with the fire of barely contained temper simmering beneath the surface. He could still walk away from that, even as intriguing as it was. But he sensed something else. Maybe it was his imagination or some kind of deep desire to connect, but he thought he saw sadness in those mystic eyes, even a sense of isolation. An outsider, not unlike him.

And that was what threatened him the most. What had put that sadness there? What had perpetrated that sense of being alone?

Shit, shit, shit!

It was a sure indication that it was time to move on. Overdue, actually. He'd been suspended in nothingness for far too long. Maybe he should gather the two or three things that meant anything to him, hop on the bike, and head north. He had no concrete ties. Especially now that things had quieted down at the Goose.

The thought roamed in his head as he rode. No, no concrete ties. No ties at all, not to mean anything, at least. But he didn't have any anywhere. He and his mom weren't close. Not really. He'd make an annual pilgrimage to see her just to be uncomfortable and awkward. He was a painful reminder of husband number two and his mother liked to reflect on how much he looked and acted like his dad. Sometimes to the point of popping an Imitrex and laying down when the migraines struck. Husband number three would slide into a melancholy sulk whenever this happened and cast pointed, accusatory stares at Luke.

Like it was his fucking fault his father died in a wreck when he was two. Like it was his fucking fault that the woman was subject to hell headaches. Sometimes he had to quell the urge to drag his stepfather up by his paisley suspenders and give him a good shake. The only thing keeping him from doing it was a detached sense of gratitude. It was mostly because of George that Luke spent so much time with his grandmother growing up. "Getting the boy out of the house" was best for a sickly and nervous woman. As an adult, it meant staying away for long spans of time until the inevitable guilt-prodding phone call came: "Why don't you come up and see your mother once in a while?"

God, it was maddening.

He supposed he had a marginally better relationship with his half-sister, but she lived in Dayton with her accountant husband, their two-point-five kids, dog, cat, white picket fence, and Slip 'N Slide. Although Tina always kept the front door symbolically unlocked, the idea of venturing too close made his teeth ache. Luke chose not to acknowledge it hurt on another, deeper level.

Hell, maybe he should try somewhere like Wyoming or Montana. Someplace with a less dense population and crisp winters, where a man could breathe.

Right.

Luke was a southern boy and he couldn't imagine living anywhere else.

The vibrant image of a smoky-eyed redhead broke through his mental ramblings once more and Luke gritted his teeth.

Allowing a low growl that echoed deep in his chest, he opted to exit the freeway and make a U-turn toward home. His brief moments of Zen were now ruined.

****

The tepid shower hadn't helped. It had sloughed off the road dust but did little to shift his mood.

Luke stared into the mirror fogged by the heat of his shower. His distorted image wavered back at him and he had the feeling that might be the true him. Hazy, disconnected, not there. A ghost of a man.

Maybe that was why he stayed in the old bar. He felt right at home. He wasn't dead, but he didn't feel like he was living either, so he split the difference.

He wasn't sure when Rowan would be back, so he hastened to shave, thoroughly rinse the sink, and pack up his toiletries. He never left a trace if he could help it.

Throwing his shirt over his shoulder, he stepped from the heated fog of the bathroom into the cool bedroom. Her bed was unmade, a tank top and pajama bottoms carelessly thrown across the foot. No long t-shirt this time. A tiny smile twisted his lips the night she'd been introduced to Robert the ghost. She had nice legs. He would have liked to see more.

Fleeting warmth turned cold and his smile morphed into a glower. Darkness pushed out the flicker of light, bringing him back into his comfort zone.

Luke started to pull his shirt on as he left the bedroom, freezing at the creak of the door.

Rowan stood inside, hand on the knob. She'd gone running. Sweat darkened her top, shining against her brow. Now staring at him through narrowed eyes, a frown crinkled her normally smooth brow. As her gaze swept over his torso, the appearance of irritation quickly dissolved, replaced by widened eyes and her mouth dropping open.

Heat bloomed under his skin and he quickly yanked the shirt over and down, blocking further perusal. With a stiff nod, he strode past her.

Luke could sense those misty eyes searing into his back as he retreated, and he could barely contain his temper when he let himself into office to start the day.

He was such a fucking idiot. He should have been more careful. It had no doubt been inevitable, but that knowledge did nothing to take the bite out of what happened.

He despised feeling so fucking vulnerable. At one time it held him in its powerful grip for months, but that was a long time ago. He thought he was done with it.

What was it about this girl that made him feel so damned exposed?

Luke booted up Jimmy's ancient CPU and opened the morning books, only to stop and stare at the far wall in thought. A tiny part of him recognized that Jimmy's swimsuit calendar had disappeared in lieu of something with Japanese woodblock prints, but most of him studied Rowan's face in retrospect. Of all the reactions he could have perceived, the one thing he didn't read from her was pity.

Chapter Ten

The low roar of dozens of conversations with the occasional guffaw overtook the crooning of Tim McGraw from the jukebox. Tim would soon be silenced in favor of live musicians as the band set up on the tiny corner platform. Christy and Taylor sped from table to table, while Luke tended the bar with efficiency she admired, even if it didn't always include a smile. Rowan had hired a couple of part-timers to help out on weekend evenings and Rowan did a quick search, finding Zoe taking an order at one of the booths, and Justin serving something fruity and colorful to an old lady dressed to match the drink.

For a moment, she caught herself drifting back to watch Luke, the memory of his scars etched permanently into her brain. Darkened skin and mottled, puckered flesh spread down his right shoulder, arm, and a third of the way across his chest.

Burns. The aftermath of second and third degree burns.

Jesus. What had happened to him?

He caught her staring and she looked away when his gaze hardened.

The band had almost finished setting up and unexpected nerves shook through her. She pulled in a deep breath to release it slowly. The tavern was busy and more people were finding their way in. It would be fine. Her gamble on live musicians would pay off.

Chanting her inner pep talk, she walked up to the bar and leaned against it. She did her best to ignore Luke, unwilling to embarrass them both.

Rowan's instincts told her he wouldn't appreciate her compassion anyway. Instead, she nodded to Justin.

She tried not to cringe as the man loped her way like a big, earnest Labrador retriever puppy. He was about her age, but had the open face and gawkiness of a high school junior. "What can I get for you, Rowan?"

And he always used her first name in every single sentence. He was one hell of a bartender though. "Mix me up a hurricane?"

"The biggest and best, just for you, Rowan." His huge baby blues held hers, grin widening as she watched. She half-expected it to engulf his whole head.

"Thank you."

"You bet, Rowan." Justin turned and she watched as he grabbed what he needed with ballet-like movements, throwing in a few smooth bottle tosses for effect as he splashed it together. He pressed an orange slice onto the edge of the glass, popped a cherry on top, and slid it toward her.

She nodded her thanks.

"Enjoy, Rowan." Justin grinned, perhaps hoping for a cookie. "Can I get you anything else, Rowan?"

Trying not roll her eyes, she shook her head and took a long sip. The hurricane was sweet and strong. She'd have to be careful.

Taking her drink with her, she sipped it as she worked her way around the room, greeting folks, laughing at perceived wittiness, making sure their food and drinks were perfect, avoiding ass-grabs, and refraining from punching said ass-grabbers.

When she returned to the bar, her drink was gone. And damn if she wasn't a little tipsy. Warmth spread to the roots of her hair and her joints and muscles felt a little more fluid than they normally would. She stared at the empty glass before placing it on the edge of the counter.

Henry appeared to her right and plopped down on

the stool beside her. His creased face lit up with pleasure. "Bonsoir, ma chère! Buy you a drink?"

"Oh, that's okay. I can get them for free." She winked at him. "I know the boss."

"Yeah, yeah. I hear she a tough one, that girl."

"Is she?"

The old man laughed, the sound raspy, but pleasant.

"Would you like another one, Rowan?" Justin gave her his high-wattage smile, and before she could answer, he'd turned to mix the next one.

It sat on the bar, dark-red and gorgeous before she even realized it. With a small shrug, she took another sip.

Henry leaned over and she could smell beer and baby powder. "What's that boy on, miss?"

"I wish I knew." She sighed and looked up to see Luke staring at her. Their eyes fused, his a lightning-filled storm at sea. A little unnerved at the intensity of his gaze, she frowned but refused to break contact. After all, it wasn't her fault she saw him without a shirt. He shouldn't have been traipsing around a woman's apartment with his lean muscles hanging out all over the place. Scarred or not, the man was chiseled and more than a little yummy.

Uh oh.

"Luke regarde en colère." Henry's face drew together, eyes narrowing into nonexistence.

"Sorry?" She pulled her gaze from Luke's to stare at Henry.

"No, no, I'm sorry. He looks mad."

"He always looks mad."

"Good reason." Henry finished his beer and signaled for Justin. "Bourbon."

"Yes, sir." He whirled to grab the old man's

drink.

"And for what reason would that be?" Curious, Rowan studied Henry, wondering what he might know.

Laughing loudly, Henry patted her shoulder. "He don't like that other boy paying attention to you."

Rowan raised both brows and took a long pull from her straw. An unsolicited warmth rose up from her belly at Henry's observation and she stifled a frown. "Why would he even care?"

The sound of fiddles filled the limited space of the bar. An accordion and acoustic guitar rounded it out into a vibrant melody. The band was off and running and the reaction was an instantaneous blend of foot tapping and hustling to the dance floor.

She was pleased to see she made the right call. She'd have to bring them back.

"Don't matter." Henry threw back his drink, climbed off the stool, and held out a hand. "Let's make him a little more jealous."

Rowan looked at the stubby, gnarled hand, puzzled. With a conscious effort, she pushed the hurricane away from her.

"You ever jitterbug, ma chère?"

"I'm not very good at dancing."

"No matter. I'll teach you." His nut-brown eyes appeared from their folds, bright with expectation.

"I don't know…"

When Henry's smile sagged a little, Rowan pushed off her stool and took his hand. She liked the little old man and couldn't bear to see his light dimming. She'd heard that his wife had passed away a few years back and The Galloping Goose was his refuge. "I can't promise any kind of grace."

"That's all right. Neither can I."

Before Rowan could ponder this admission, the

old man yanked her toward the dance floor. "I'll be dancing with the prettiest girl here."

She smiled at him when he pulled her into steps as alien as any foreign language. He whirled her around with the exuberance of a younger man, before holding her close for a moment.

Henry twirled her again and she almost lost her balance, laughing, and a tiny bit drunk. When she knocked into the solid wall of flesh, Rowan almost fell a second time, but strong fingers caught her by the upper arms and she glanced up at the man's face.

Luke stared at her, face and eyes blank. She wanted to take a step back, her flesh tingling under his hands, but pride kept her in place to jut out her jaw. This man worked for her and she wasn't about to be intimidated by him.

He looked over her head and nodded to Henry. "This girl's lucky you didn't twist her arms off. Seriously, man, what was that?"

"I am the best of the best." Henry hiccupped and burped.

"The best at what? Maiming your partners?"

The old man scowled, but good humor oozed from around it. "You gonna show this old Cajun how it's done, boy?"

Luke hesitated and Henry's scowl morphed into the happy grin he'd been trying to hide.

"C'mon. You know you want to. Jolie jeune fille comme ça." He turned to the crowd, his voice rising. "Il doit avoir peur!"

Laughter rippled through the small crowd, with a few folks looking as blank as Rowan felt.

"Embrasse moi tchew," the younger man muttered, but a smile pulled at the corner of Luke's mouth.

Rowan frowned and blinked. The exchange sounded insulting, but she knew both men were clearly fond of one another, even if she couldn't comprehend why. She tried to pull away from him, uncomfortable with the shift. Dancing with the harmless little old man was one thing, but she didn't care to get cheek to cheek, or in their case, cheek to chest, with Luke.

His hands firmed, preventing her escape and she gritted her teeth.

"I don't think this is a good idea." She didn't want to cause a scene, especially as a relative newcomer in her own place. The sudden increase in her pulse didn't impress her either.

He naturally ignored her and she entertained driving her heel into his instep.

"Give your customers what they want," Luke murmured. "Just follow my lead."

Trapped, she clamped down on her discomfort. Pasting on a fake smile, she hissed between her teeth. "I'd fire you if I could."

His smile was grim. "I don't even doubt it, ma chère."

"I'm not your 'dear.'"

"Oh, you finally caught that, did you? Good for you. Maybe there's hope."

Before she could kick him in the shin, he twirled her and brought her back to catch her around the waist with one hand, seizing her fingers and pressing against her palm with his. He pulled her toward him and then propelled her back, swung her around with his arm locked at her waist, and then changed direction. Rowan let her gaze drop to his feet, startled at the ease of his quick steps.

"Look at me."

She did, finding his midnight-blue eyes locked on

her, and she managed to follow the dance through the skill of his moves. The band set the pace, the accordionist taking the lead, the fiddle players and the guitarist building the tune into an infectious blend.

"What the hell did you two say, anyhow?" Rowan was pleased to find her voice steady.

He twirled her around, his mouth pulling to the side.

"Well?"

"He accused me of being afraid to dance with you and I told him to kiss my ass."

Rowan didn't have time to analyze the exchange. Heart racing, her breath puffed from her. Dizzy, she couldn't tell if it was the alcohol or the dance. He pulled her close, spun her around and around. A laugh popped from her before she could bite it back. She wasn't positive, but she thought she caught the quick glint of his white teeth. It was gone before she could be sure.

When the music stopped, Luke didn't release her and stood perfectly still watching her. His eyes wide, they flitted between hers. Lightheaded, she stared back, warmth rushing her face, too aware of the coiled strength under her hands. Mud filled her brain and she couldn't connect words, let alone full thoughts.

The cacophony of too many people in too small a space swirled around them, converging together and shifting into white noise.

Her heart galloped in her ears, her body trembling with its intensity, but her gaze remained twined with his. Those amazing dark eyes of his shimmered in heat and something more for the longest moment before his face crumpled.

Dropping his hands from her, Luke turned his back and walked away.

Rowan blinked and almost fell, mentally shaking

herself off. A thin sheen of sweat touched her forehead and she figured her face was flushed. The AC probably needed some tweaking again.

He had disappeared behind the bar and now served a draft with a full head to a burly bearded man dwarfing the tiny stool under his butt. Luke didn't bother to look her way again.

Bewildered and annoyed at herself because of it, Rowan dodged and worked her way to the front entry. A little air would flush away the alcohol haze and maybe steady her a little.

Someone caught her by the arm, and she whirled to find Margie's gaze locked on her, a tiny frown weaving around her eyes. "Are you all right?"

Rowan forced a smile. "I'm sorry. I didn't realize you were here."

"I only just got here, honey. You look upset."

"No, no. I'm … fine. Just need a little air. The crowd's getting to me all of a sudden." She peeled the older woman's hand away, taking a moment to give it a reassuring pat. "I'll be right back."

Rowan wove around a few more people before she was able to pull the heavy door open and slide out the front. Sidestepping to avoid getting smacked at the entry, she leaned near the narrow block wall of glass and tried to rein herself in.

Her heart pounded in her temples, blood rushing heavy and hot. Sweat coated her face and trickled down the small of her back. Night air dropping into the low sixties rushed in, but relief was slow, achingly slow.

"What's the matter with me?" she murmured, the words not even reaching her through primal senses gone awry. Luke had her twisted around and baffled, and it shouldn't have even been an issue. The man was rude, aloof, damaged, and couldn't even stand her. Why did a simple dance throw her into such a tangled mess?

In that moment, she wished she hadn't come to Louisiana. She should have sold the damned tavern instead of hauling herself almost 2000 miles to deal with an asshole employee and a haunted bar.

Haunted.

The jury was still out on that one. Her logical brain continued to vie for a reasonable explanation, sure it could be found.

Her emotions told her another story, but she endeavored to squash it.

Closing her eyes, she pressed her hand to her forehead, expecting it would be pulsing under her fingertips, relieved when it wasn't. Tomorrow she would call her parents. Just to check in, hear their voices, even if her mother annoyed her.

"You okay, pretty lady?"

Rowan nodded and good manners stifled the urge to tell the Samaritan to go away and be concerned about someone else.

"Sure? You look a little pale."

She cracked her eyes open, any words lost in a gasp. Jerking backward, she flattened her body against the block glass, inadvertently smacking the back of her head. A spin of dizziness chased a few painful sparkles around her until she blinked it away.

The green-eyed man stood less than three feet from her. He tilted his head and smiled. "Ah, you're a difficult one, oui?"

"Who are you?"

"An acquaintance of your uncle's." He slid one foot forward and his face filled her vision. "His death was very unfortunate for me, but then voilà! Here you are. It's important for family to take care of family, do you not think so?"

"I don't know what the hell you're talking about." Rowan kept her voice from shaking and considered it a small victory. Her next victory would be kneeing him in the balls, if at all possible, but her body felt too heavy, too ineffectual. "What do you want from me?"

"I guess this is all very confusing for you, but it doesn't matter. I'll make it simple." He leaned in and she thought she could smell smoke on his breath. "Your uncle owed me. I lost him, so the debt is yours."

"I don't have a lot of money…"

The man opened his mouth and laughed. "Well, that's unfortunate, but there are other ways to pay a debt—"

"Rowan? You okay?"

She swiveled her head to find Justin popping out the front door, goggling at her, and the man who should have still been in her periphery, gone. Nauseated, Rowan bent from the waist and rested her palms on her knees. "Did you see anyone?" Her voice sounded unfamiliar to her own ears, wispy, weak, strength gone.

And it pissed her off.

His brow crinkled, pink rising from his neck. "Um … well, I think a few people may have left."

"You didn't see the guy that was standing here a second ago?" She looked up at him, concentrating on her breathing. Slow and steady.

He opened his mouth and closed it again, befuddled.

"Never mind." Straightening, she pushed past him on shaky legs and slid back into the throngs of people. The warmth of the tavern settled around her and for the first time, she took comfort from it.

Chapter Eleven

As he worked pouring neat liquor, mixing cocktails, and drawing drafts, his mind kept wandering and Luke found himself keeping an eye out for Rowan. She'd left the tavern a little too quickly and now concern scrubbed against his brain. He didn't like her out there alone at night.

His heart hadn't slowed despite effort to pull in and steady his breathing. Sense memory still had her in his arms, the scent of her light fragrance in his nose, the unguarded surprise in her eyes. It had taken everything he had to walk away.

And now all he wanted was to kick the shit out of himself. Okay, first Henry, then himself. As much as he liked the old man, Luke could have cheerfully killed him in his sleep over that little stunt.

His gaze found its way back to the entry, but still no Rowan.

Wiping his hands on a towel, he took several steps to clear the bar, stopping when that kid Justin pushed outside first. No doubt he was just doing the same damn thing Luke had intended.

Anger and displeasure crept up his spine. Gritting his teeth, the muscles in his jaw throbbed. What difference could it possibly even make? That guy could make a play for her, she could reciprocate, and all of a sudden, Luke's life would become a whole lot easier.

Naturally, he told himself a fanciful lie even while his subconscious whispered the truth. Every misgiving he held was slowly being pummeled under new affection and new desire. And it scared the shit out of him. He still associated those tender feelings with loss, and he doubted it could ever change. It would always stand as a blockade to happiness for him.

Despite himself, when Rowan reappeared, Luke subtly craned his neck to watch her, frowning. Her face bloodless, she pushed past Justin as if he weren't there and now worked her way through the crowd. She couldn't have been more than five-four, so it was easy to lose her. He did manage to catch a glimpse of her red hair or flash of the bright turquoise of her blouse though.

Settling into a booth, she squeezed into the corner, back to the wall, face still wan. Hell, she looked downright sick. It cut him straight to the heart, but he refrained going over when Margie slid in next to her. The older woman tilted her head, brows drawn together. Her lips moved in conversation lost to him.

"Can't keep your eyes off her, can you, mon ami?"

Luke walked back behind the bar and shook his head. "Henry, you see more than what's there."

The old man clucked a tongue and downed his shot, waving him away when Luke went to refill. "Beautiful girl."

"Lots of pretty women out there." Luke responded, his voice tight.

"Not always the right ones though." Henry kept his eyes steady on him, and something in that stare reminded Luke that this wasn't just any old man. This was a man who'd experienced all sides of life from the cradle to the gutter to Vietnam to now. His wife had been with him for forty-eight years and now he visited the lovingly maintained crypt that neighbored the daughter they'd lost at the age of three. He'd worked as a bricklayer most of his post-war life, with scars and callouses to prove it, had taken painting classes for love, if lack of talent. He still lived in the same little shotgun house he and his wife had shared, the same place they'd raised

Andy. And he still tended to his wife's garden, filled with begonias, lilies, and honeysuckle, despite her being gone close to six years.

Shame flooded Luke again and he said nothing.

"How old are you, Lukas?"

"Thirty-four. Why?"

Those brown eyes stayed on his, searching, knowing, despite the alcohol he'd ingested. "The rest of your life is a long time to mourn."

Within the cacophony of the tavern, the moment spread as only similar commonality could between two men. Finally, it broke and Henry reached out to slap Luke's bicep when he didn't respond. "I think it's time for me to get lost and get my old ass to bed."

Yanking his wallet from his trousers, the old man counted out some bills and tossed them on the bar. "Bonsoir, mon ami."

"Night, Henry."

****

The last of her customers gone, Rowan locked the front door and leaned against it. The time she'd spent hiding in the corner and brooding had only served to sharpen her determination and temper. She wasn't a weak little woman and resented being made to feel that way.

She'd questioned Margie about any … unusual … debts Jimmy may have had, but the lawyer couldn't really help her. What registered on the books were the usual credits cards and a small loan he'd taken out to fix the plumbing a couple years back. Nothing else to her knowledge.

So, whatever it was, it was something her uncle had kept close to his chest.

It crossed her mind she could go to the police regarding the green-eyed man, but realized she didn't have much to offer. He gave off a creepy vibe, which, although disturbing, was far from illegal. He had yet to come out and officially threaten her, choosing to taunt her instead. No. He had a plan. Those eyes were intelligent, cunning. She couldn't fathom what it might be, though.

And that scared her.

Debts paid by means other than money led to too many dark imaginings. Her brain remained fertile with possibilities.

A shudder quaked through her and Rowan stepped from the entry to haul chairs up and over the sides of tables. Taylor nodded and smiled a thanks as she did the same. Zoe appeared, dragging the ancient vacuum cleaner, and they all jumped when its growl filled the room.

Christy had elected to help Sonny out with the kitchen, while Justin cleaned the bar. She'd occasionally catch him watching her, only to look away when she met his eye.

With all of them pitching in, it took little time to whip the place back into shape, and Rowan soon found herself walking her staff to the back door to wish them all a good night.

Only then, did she seek Luke out.

She leaned in the doorway of the office, eying him, irked at the allure of his fluid grace. He'd finished the night's books and had gotten up to drop the deposit, and now turned, brows raised. "Problem?"

"No, that would be your department. I did have a couple of things I wanted to ask you, though." Rowan snapped, not in the mood for his attitude.

Saying nothing, he leaned back against the desk and crossed his arms. His dark-blue gaze stared, impassive.

"Well, gosh boss, what did you need? How can I help?"

Not rising to her sarcasm, he continued to watch her.

Rowan closed her eyes for a moment and opened them to bite back a frustrated scream. Counting back from twenty, she let out a slow breath. "Do you know anything about my uncle's debts?"

He tilted his head and frowned. "I would think you'd have all that information, considering you inherited everything he had."

The fierce tone had her blinking. "I meant anything ... not above board."

Luke stared at her through simmering eyes. "You think Jimmy was a crook?"

Blood rushed to her face when her temper surged. She held onto it, but spoke from between her teeth. "No. I wondered if he accidentally got himself into something he shouldn't have. Gambling, maybe? Did he owe money ... or whatever ... to someone he shouldn't have?"

Something shifted in his face, so quick and subtle there was no way she could identify it.

"Not that I know of." He straightened. "Jimmy was a proud man, a good man. I don't think he'd appreciate your suspicions. If you don't mind, boss, I'm tired and I'd like to get a few hours of sleep."

Luke strode by her, flipping off the light.

She stood for a moment, back stiffening, before her temper slid out from under its thin lid. "What the hell is your problem? I've done nothing to you."

"Good. Keep on doing it." Luke pulled the office door shut and turned down the hallway. "I don't need some spoiled brat looking over my shoulder or ruining Jimmy's business."

Red bled behind her eyes and her temper boiled

over. "Spoiled? You know nothing about me. I'd probably be disowned several times over if were up to my mother. Whatever I have, I've scraped together on my own. And now I'm just a damned gypsy living in my dead uncle's apartment. You have a lot of gall judging me. What is even the matter with you? What kind of loser lives in a storeroom in a bar?" She pulled in a breath, lashing out before she could think better of it, a flare of fire blinding her to the sting on his face.

"The kind that doesn't need any of your fucking questions."

"Like it or not, we have an employee-employer relationship. Could we at least try to be civil?" Pulling in several deep breaths, she tried to calm herself even as her face burned and muscles clenched. Frustrated tears stung her eyes, but there was no way she'd give him the satisfaction of seeing them fall. "Or could it be you just don't like working for a woman?"

"You don't know what you're talking about."

"The hell I don't! You wouldn't be the first man to find issue with it."

"Bullshit."

"Then tell me what the problem is."

"Why are you even following me?" He spat out, ignoring her words, face granite as he approached his room.

Rowan stopped short. He'd pushed the door open and his single bed crowded the far corner. He stared at her, eyes burning with cold temper before his face twisted into an ugly sneer.

"Maybe you feel the need to take a tumble with the help, huh? Maybe do a little slumming, ma chère?"

The insult was so brazen, so outrageous, she didn't even think. Balling her fist, she struck out fast and hard to connect with the corner of his mouth. "Bastard."

Luke's head snapped to the right. When he turned back to her, something dangerous lurked in his dark-blue eyes. Unease cooled her insides, and she suddenly became very aware that they were the only two people in the building. Swallowing, she took an inadvertent step backward. Pride screamed for her to stop, but self-preservation prodded her to run.

She glanced toward the stairwell and took another step back, her fury having disappeared into mist. She'd always been warned her temper would get her in trouble, and it occurred to her that this was a prime example. Luke was a big man, easily six-two and 180 pounds of lean muscle. He could hurt her without breaking a sweat.

Edging away, she continued to watch him warily. She wanted to run but didn't think she could get away if he chose to lash out. Something close to terror quivered low in her belly.

They said nothing for several long moments, tension stretching and tearing. He seemed to wrestle with something deep inside, something she doubted she would ever be privy to.

Finally, he sighed, long and resigned. "I deserved that. I was out of line. I'm sorry."

Rowan eyed him, surprised at his apology but still suspicious. Her fingers curled around the door frame, knuckles white.

Stepping away, Luke dropped his gaze. "If there's nothing else that needs to be done, I'm going to get some sleep." He turned to retreat into his room, shutting the door behind him.

Still shaking, Rowan stood in the hallway for a long moment, clenching and unclenching her fists. His sudden shift confused the hell out of her. He'd gone from predatory taunting to dangerous fury to what? Luke's expression had fallen into such sadness it made her chest ache.

She stared at the closed door for a bit longer, before making up her mind and heading toward the kitchen.

****

He'd refrained from slamming the door, but barely. A ten by twenty room, half-filled with supplies and assorted junk didn't allow it for long. He dropped to do pushups instead and kept going until his arms trembled, burned, and he lost count.

Fucking asshole.

He'd never threatened a woman in his life, but Rowan had absorbed his exasperation, misinterpreting it into something much more dark and insidious.

Jesus.

He wouldn't have noticed the knock, but he had stopped his impromptu workout moments before. Debating the ramifications of ignoring it, he knew he couldn't. Luke swiped a forearm across his brow and took three steps to open the door. Rowan stood in the hallway holding a bag of frozen vegetables and a damp washcloth.

Luke shifted his gaze from her face to her hands and back again. "You brought me peas?"

"I have a pretty impressive right hook." Her voice held gentle surrender as she shrugged.

"Yeah, I felt that." Touched and surprised by her gesture, he took the offered bag and held it gingerly to his chin.

Rowan continued to linger in the doorway, before allowing a resigned sigh. "I'm sorry. I should never have hit you. I lost my temper."

Luke felt his lips twitch. She looked so uncomfortable with her admission but genuinely guilty at the same time. "The pop was justified. You don't owe me an apology."

"Here. You're bleeding." Pressing her mouth into a straight line, she stepped into the room, holding out the cloth. She gently swiped the corner of his mouth, brows pulled together to form a tiny pucker between. He read concern in her beautiful eyes and unnamed emotion swelled inside his chest.

Luke sucked in a breath and held it while his heart kicked into a rolling gallop. Not allowing himself to analyze the motion, he reached up and curled his fingers around her wrist. It felt fine-boned and delicate, but the underlying strength was unmistakable. He brushed a thumb to the inside, the skin so soft and smooth.

Rowan took a half-step back. "What are you doing?"

Gently, he pushed her hand away. "Goodnight, Ms. O'Herley."

She didn't move, only staring up at him, the dark mist of her eyes flashing. "You know you're maddening, don't you? I think hitting you was inevitable."

He twisted his mouth into a pained smile. "Probably."

"It was either that or—" She cut herself off and edged away.

"Or what?" He balanced the distance between them, his hands reaching toward hers before he realized it. He let them drop back to his sides.

"Nothing."

Shit, shit, shit. The underlying pull burned beneath his flesh. God, he wanted her. He kept so still, his body trembled. Why wouldn't she just go already? But no, she stood her ground, now eyeing him as if solving a puzzle.

Lust had to have been reverberating from him in thick waves, but instead of turning, running like a normal woman might in view of the situation, she stood her ground and stared up at him, accessing.

"You're such an enigma. Who are you, really, Luke Meunier?" she murmured, looking up at him with those shining pewter eyes.

Oh, hell. Luke caught her by the upper arms and pulled her to her toes. He hesitated only a moment before covering her mouth with his. He felt her stiffen for the barest of moments, then her fluid warmth as her lips slid into perfect synchronicity with his. He lost the sting of his minor injury in a haze of desire. A tingle of energy pulsed through him when he wrapped his arms around her slim waist, distantly aware of her hands cupping his face and sifting into his hair.

The red need of primal want burned under his skin, having him a bit lightheaded when all his blood ran south. Her mouth was so soft and formed to his. He didn't know if he could keep himself from pushing to explore the rest of her smooth skin and curves, but with one final scraping of her lower lip, he broke away and stepped back.

Her fair skin flushed and eyes darkened, she blinked, backed away, looking anywhere but at him. Her tongue flicked out in a tiny lip lick and his desire surged once more. He gritted his teeth to keep his passion from taking control.

"Um, I … goodnight," Rowan backed away, hit the wall, twisted around, and left.

****

Rowan told herself she hadn't run away, she'd simply walked away. It had been a long night and she needed to get some sleep.

At the top of the stairs, she dropped to her butt

and pressed her hands to her scorching face.

Who the hell was she kidding?

Of course she'd ran. Somehow, someway, everything had slid out of control and she didn't remember when she'd allowed it to happen.

She'd almost admitted that hitting or kissing him was inevitable, but bit it back, but Jesus. She'd done both. Of course, technically he'd kissed her first, but she hadn't exactly stopped him. Touching her fingers to her lips, the feel of his gentle warmth lingered.

No. It was just one of those things. Her emotions, her fears, all of it pent up inside, no wonder she'd popped off like that. He'd provoked her on purpose. That much was obvious.

And she'd called him a loser.

Mortification and regret burned her cheeks and she dropped her face forward onto her folded arms.

Major jerk move on her part. Her comment had been cruel and heartless. By nature, she wasn't normally that kind of person and couldn't imagine why he brought it out in her. She knew nothing of his choices or the reasoning behind them. There had to be something major lurking in his past.

Tears filled her eyes and flowed in stealth. Silent sobs shook her shoulders as grief overtook her. Rowan let go.

She cried for an uncle she remembered as a warm and gentle giant with a big, bellowing laugh, wearing the kitty ears she'd favored at six. She cried over an old building she'd inherited that was so much more than what she could have ever expected. She cried over an angry, abrasive, and scarred man with a touch and kiss so achingly tender she felt like she'd thrown open a cellar door to a different dimension.

And she cried over the fact that she had

absolutely no idea what the hell she was doing or what she'd somehow landed in.

She'd promised herself she would stick it out, but with a tiny sliver of withering fortitude, began to wonder if was worth it. Mom and Daddy would welcome her in delight with only a limited amount of "I told you so." Maybe.

No, she couldn't … wouldn't … do that. Despite everything, she felt a pull toward this new adopted city of hers with its unique energy, and she was compelled to get to know it even better.

The scent of roses swirled around her and she shook her head, smiling as her tears continued to fall. "I think, Mavis, you must have been a mother."

The presence intensified, aroma thickening. For the briefest of moments, Rowan could have sworn someone squeezed her shoulder. With tentative fingers and a shaking hand, she reached up to cool air and nothing more.

"I appreciate the effort, although I probably look pretty pathetic from your point of view." She felt foolish, but since the perfume didn't dissipate, she continued. "To be honest, I guess I can handle Luke. But I'm not so sure what to do about … the other one. I'm afraid I might even be imagining him. No one else seems to see him."

The atmosphere hugging her dropped in temperature until she could see her breath, before a violent wind whipped it away, rushing through her hair and bringing thick peaks of gooseflesh to her skin.

An instant later, the presence was gone, leaving Rowan's heart stuttering and her body trembling. "What was that?"

She sat in the dark a few moments longer before giving up and pushing up to legs a little too wobbly.

Chapter Twelve

No sleep and two cups of coffee brought Rowan downstairs when sunlight was still a smudge on the horizon. Going for a run crossed her mind, but the thought didn't catch hold. She had a feeling she'd collapse before the half-mile mark.

For the hell of it, she popped a couple of coins in the jukebox and chose some old Motown to get her moving. She could have grabbed the key from the office, but laziness cozied with exhaustion.

Pulling chairs down, she lined them up under tables, figuring she'd save her staff the trouble later. She also wanted to do a count to see if she needed to replenish any inventory. After last night, she expected as much.

Walking past the bar into the kitchen, she nosed through the industrial-size fridge and freezer before browsing through the pantry. She checked the unofficial list Sonny had scribbled and tacked inside the door, thinking they might have a few supplies in Luke's room. Rowan figured she'd worry about that later.

Humming along with Dianna Ross, she stepped back to the front of the tavern and couldn't quite stifle a short squawk. Staring, she pressed her hands to her mouth, eyes wide.

Every chair she'd pulled down had been flipped around to hook back over the edge of every single table.

Her heart sung loud and persistent in her chest.

Rowan moved in a slow circle, listening and watching for anyone nearby. Maybe Luke was up and screwing with her, but even as she thought it, she didn't think it was his style.

She was so damned tired, she could have

imagined she'd rearranged the furniture. As she considered, that seemed the most feasible explanation.

Grabbing each chair, she tucked them under the tables a second time and headed toward the hall to see about the night's deposit. Armored transport would be by later that morning and she wanted to double-check everything was as it should be. She also wanted to do a little research to see what it might set her back to pull down that ugly dark paneling in the front. With any luck, there'd be more of that lovely original brick hiding behind it.

Stopping, she almost fell, the squawk elevating to a short scream.

She hated screaming, but she gaped at the chairs now lined along the wall opposite the office.

"What the hell is this?" Rowan couldn't seem to bring oxygen to her lungs and pressed a heavy hand to her chest. Twisting around, she ran to the front to find every chair lined with every table.

She returned to the hall.

The chairs were gone.

"Shit, shit, shit." Rowan leaned against the wall and her legs gave out to send her sliding to the worn tile.

"What the hell is this?" she asked the air again. Something occurred to her and she clenched her jaw. Finding her show of temper ridiculous, she was helpless to rein it in.

"Robert? C'mon, give me a break. If this is you, I'd appreciate you quitting this shit."

No sudden blast of cold this time. No breaking of glass.

She sighed. Maybe she was tipping the scales toward insanity. Maybe intricate nightmares in her mind were overflowing into the outside world to blur the line between sanity and insanity.

Rowan dropped her elbows on her knees and hung her head. Tears had flooded from her in a torrent the previous night and now she felt hollow. She vaguely wondered how long it would be before she shattered, dissolved and poofed out into the atmosphere.

Ashes to ashes, dust to dust.

Clamping her teeth on her inner cheek, she bit back a hysterical giggle.

As far as she could tell, there was no reality here, only slips of the mind and swirls of shadows in her consciousness. Everything she thought she knew had crumbled away, at least that was how it seemed.

A sudden outer chill flowed over her, persistent and pervasive.

She shuddered and closed her eyes.

****

Luke shoved through the door off the stairwell and stepped into the hall. Worry burned through his gut when his restless gaze tracked over to find Rowan puddled on the floor. Images from the previous evening had plagued his sleep throughout the night and he'd finally decided it had been nothing more than a mistake. Even as he continued to lie to himself, he deliberately approached, keeping his face cool, words clipped. "What are you doing?"

"It's comfortable down here." She didn't look at him, just stared at the floor, forearms on knees, hands dangling. "Go away."

He raised his brows, only to crinkle them as he studied her. Her pallor looked ashen, shadows etching deep half-moons under her eyes. Hair that had been pulled back into a ponytail, escaped in wispy strands to hang over her face, and a sheen of perspiration coated her brow.

A brief but intense memory struck him and a cold

ball of fear began to weave its way to form a dense knot in his belly.

No. No way could history be repeating. It didn't make sense.

Clenching his teeth, Luke left and returned a few seconds later to crouch down beside her. He offered the glass of iced water without comment.

Rowan stared at him for a long moment before accepting the glass with a murmured "thanks." Her hand shook and she used the other to steady it. "Does, uh, Robert ever rearrange the furniture?"

"What?"

"Never mind."

"Did something happen?" He frowned down at her, and after a moment, she shook her head.

"Don't you have somewhere to be?" Her words should have held bite, but instead they lacked energy, closing in on monotone.

"I do, actually. But if you're having some kind of issue, I'd rather hang out. I don't want you screwing anything up."

The slow turn of her head had her stare hardening. A muscle in her jaw throbbed.

There. That's better.

"Piss off."

Luke smirked to throw a little kerosene on the embers. Her lips tightened and a flush spread across her face to push out the gray pallor.

Satisfied, he straightened. "I'm going to go grab a shower. If you decide to have a breakdown in the next fifteen minutes, try to hold off."

"Jerk." She climbed to her feet, glaring at him, and without a word, pushed past him to walk toward the office.

****

Luke parked the bike, stripped off his gear, and began to walk.

He made the pilgrimage every few months, two lavender chrysanthemums and one tiny buff-colored teddy bear in hand.

It was still early, and aside from passing traffic, the grounds were quiet. Greenery met intricately carved stone, somber instead of infused with the peace they attempted to portray. Not that it was their fault. It was what it was.

He shoved one hand in the pocket of his jeans, unhurried in his pace, but his mind remained frenetic. He passed the fountain before weaving through catacombs into marble hallways.

Not far. Just at the end, conveniently near the wooden bench where his knees used to sometimes give out. It hadn't happened in a while, but they'd still threaten to liquefy if memories overtook him.

He stopped before the etched names, reaching out to trace them with his fingers.

It was an old habit. Maybe it was still denial, but at his point he doubted it. It had turned into a comfort thing. Nothing more, nothing less.

Catherine Louise Meunier

McKenzie Lynn Meunier

Cate had always hated her middle name.

"They just had to name me after Uncle Louis. A sweet man with bulging eyes and a turkey wattle."

Luke smiled at the memory. She'd been smiling at the time as well. She'd loved her uncle, poultry appendage and all.

He placed the two flowers in the vase, propping the teddy behind them. They'd be gone by his next visit, but each and every time, he hoped the bear found a loving home with another child.

"Almost three years now." In one month and twenty-one days. He calculated it every single moment of his life. "I guess I'll never understand why some spirits stay around and others move on. Is it about youth? Purity? Does fire cleanse? Or is it only the good ones that automatically move on?"

Silence sunk in around him, traffic too distant, any other unseen visitors stuck in their own contemplative meditation.

Luke sighed and dropped down on the bench, his gaze still on both names. "Jesus, Caty, I don't even know what to do any more. I miss you so damned much, but I'm withering into nothing here."

He shoved a hand through his hair and gave it a frustrated tug. "You probably wouldn't even recognize me anymore. I live in a fucking bar, hide from everyone, even when I'm out there on display. None of the guys come around anymore. Brayden, John, Arnie, not even Russ. Not that I can blame them. Who wants to hang out with a husk? Can't go back, even if I wanted to. Did I ever tell you that? The psychological bullshit ended it."

Silence. No frigid breeze. No touch of her perfume in the air. No fragrance from Kenzie's lavender baby bath.

He cupped his face, scrubbed his hands down. "It doesn't really matter though. None of it. I thought I'd accepted it all, though, figuring there wasn't anything left for me. I always figured I had one shot, you know? I always figured no one can ever replace you or our beautiful baby girl.

"And that still stands. Of course no one can take your place. I love you dearly. I'll always love you, but now I'm wondering if I might have room for someone else in my life." Luke leaned back, letting his hands drop between his knees. "It makes me feel like shit, and I guess it's kind of fucked up to admit this to you, Cate, but I can't keep this woman out of my head now. God, I try. So fucking hard. But there she is, always around, always, just there. Physically, sure, I mean I work with her, eh, actually, who the fuck am I kidding? I work for her. But even when she's not there, I'm thinking about her. I even considered pulling up stakes and finally getting the hell out of New Orleans, but I can't seem to do it. I think she might be having … some troubles and you know how I am about damsels in distress."

He shook his head with a hesitant smile. "Not that she really fits that role. Too headstrong, temperamental, too much of a pain in the ass to consider herself in need of rescue. Or maybe she's even here to rescue me. Go figure that one."

"But you want to know the ironic part?" His smile melted away. "I doubt she even likes me. God knows I haven't given her any reason to. To be honest, I've been a bastard to her from the second she stepped into The Goose. But when I'm with her, something, a tiny piece of me, unfreezes and comes back to life."

Luke leaned back, tilting his head against the wall behind him. Tears seared his eyes, but didn't fall.

"… and I don't understand it."

Chapter Thirteen

Rowan opted for a healthy serving of "screw that asshole" with a side dish of "I'm carrying pepper spray and would be delighted to use it."

During the crystalline day with its cheerful, puffy white clouds, the memory of her stalker elicited anger instead of fear. She'd be damned if she'd be made a prisoner in her own place.

After getting sidetracked for weeks, she finally found her way to the closest library to satiate her curiosity and perhaps even gather some answers. With the help of an enthusiastic library page, she was able to dig out old records and information about the building she'd inherited.

Margie wasn't too far off. It had been built in 1806, initially as a bank. Slightly less than forty years later, it was sold and renovated into a high-end restaurant. After that, a mercantile.

There was nothing of interest or note until it was purchased by a wealthy Frenchman named Charles Le Gall, who refurbished the building specifically for his young creole bride. Josephine Le Gall moved in shortly after renovations and the couple moved in high-end social circles, appearing happy to all concerned. She gave birth to their first child, a boy, a year later. Two years after that, she bore Charles a daughter.

Rowan frowned as she read, a see-saw of nausea pitching low in her belly. It would seem the Le Galls weren't destined for a happily-ever-after. The little boy contracted cholera, dying a couple days before his seventh birthday. Distraught, Charles fell into a deep depression, ignoring his wife and daughter, locking himself away in his office. On the evening on June 17,

1872, the man's sanity snapped and he attempted to kill the little girl with a butcher knife. Josephine intervened, taking the blade in the heart to save her daughter.

Charles Le Gall came back to himself shortly after, horrified by what he'd done. He fled the house, made his way to the cemetery where his son was interred, and committed suicide by stabbing himself in the chest with the same knife he'd inadvertently killed his wife. The daughter, Amelia, was sent to live with Josephine's sister. From everything Rowan read, the little girl lived a long and successful life as an artist and early feminist.

The building changed hands several more times over the years, becoming another restaurant, an art gallery, briefly even a brothel, before it landed as a bar sometime in the mid-twentieth century. Three more deaths occurred within that time span: two heart attacks and one shooting by a jealous husband.

And then Jimmy. But of course he wasn't listed in the history.

Shuddering, Rowan pulled her gaze away. Sometimes ignorance really was bliss.

Determined to shake off the veil of unease, Rowan left the library on foot to catch the streetcar down to the Spanish Plaza by the river. She decided to spend the afternoon people watching, listening to live music, and poking through shops at the outlet mall. In light of the beauty around her, the darkness of her research and current existence gradually lifted.

Los Angeles carried its own energy, but the sprawl managed to mute it to white noise, whereas New Orleans held distinct spikes in its own unique flavor. Rowan loved it.

There was no sign of the green-eyed man, but she kept watch, almost hoping for an appearance. All her pent-up frustrations were looking for an outlet and she really wanted to hurt him if she could.

For several moments, she considered taking a tour on the paddle wheeler, but figured that would be for another time. Maybe a cruise at night would even be fun. Dixie, dinner, and dancing. Huh. It definitely had merit. The idea of taking a river boat down the Mississippi appealed to her romantic nature.

New thoughts threatened to intrude. Luke's visage and new emotions she refused to entertain tried to torment, but she shook them off like a wet dog. It didn't matter. Rowan had always enjoyed her own company. Now was no different.

She glanced at her watch and winced before deciding it might be time to head back. Luke would have already opened the tavern for lunch and the impending happy hour. There was no doubt in her mind he'd make a comment about her absence. But it wasn't really his business. If she was going to be stuck with him anyway, he may as well do his job.

Dodging around and through clumps of other pedestrians, she headed past the Toulouse streetcar, in favor of the one that ran along Canal. Rowan felt a kindling of pride as her confidence in her navigation grew.

She climbed aboard, found a seat next to the window, and waited.

Too many other folks crammed on as well and Rowan found herself surrounded by a group of tourists. She still held too much in common and couldn't imagine getting to the point where the streetcar would become blasé. Listening to the happy chatter around her, she eyeballed her watch again, figuring she had more than enough time to get back before the after-work shift started its nightly migration into The Galloping Goose.

"If you take this to the end, I think you get to see

some of the local cemeteries," a heavy-set woman in her early fifties, wearing a bright yellow sundress, informed her seat companion. "Remember, they don't bury them here."

"Well, that's disturbing. Why not?" The other woman, of similar age and build, wore a velour jogging set. She pulled her digital camera from the depths of her purse and snapped a few of the car's interior.

"Low sea level. They'd get flooded out. I read during Katrina there were caskets floating all over the place."

"Oh, God." Velour took a couple of photos of a palm tree before squishing her face together in disgust at her companion.

"I guess they call it one of the most haunted cities in the country for a reason."

"Got that right," Rowan muttered, watching a couple of kids on skateboards jump curbs as the streetcar passed.

One voice lowered in conspiracy, this one male. "I heard one was actually screaming."

"Really? How could that be?" Velour woman gasped.

"Buried alive. I've read that happens here."

"Those are just stories." The woman's voice betrayed her doubtful response. "I think you watch too many movies."

Rowan shifted, uncomfortable. Too many films and books in her own right led a little credence to the discussion floating on either side of her.

"You know what I heard once?" Another male voice, New York thickening his accent. "Sometimes there'd be hits put on people and they'd turn them into real-life zombies."

"Oh, c'mon, Carl! That's ridiculous!"

"Honest. That's what I heard. This voodoo hocus-pocus stuff has some serious followers."

Ice slid into Rowan's veins and she considered getting off at the next stop. In light of recent events, she knew her imagination would suck this information up and spit it out at her in her dreams. A shudder quaked through her and she figured it might be wise to bring ear buds and music for her next city excursion.

"Do you know what happens to little girls who don't fulfill their family obligations?"

A strong hand grabbed her by the arm and she yanked away with a gasp. "What?"

For the flicker of a moment, the man leaning over from the seat before her flashed intense and angry green eyes. She blinked and his gaze melted into warm chocolate syrup. "Are you okay, miss?"

"What?" She repeated, staring. Sun-kissed fair skin instead of smooth mocha. The man before her was easily into his sixties with a shock of white hair combed back from his brow, and glasses perched on the end of his long nose.

"Honey?" One of the women behind her switched seats and pressed a gentle hand to shoulder. "Are you okay? Can we call someone for you?"

The streetcar came to a stop, and shaking her head, Rowan got up to push past. Too many people kept inquiring about her welfare of late. She knew they meant well, but she wanted the circumstances eliciting her well-wishes to stop. Enough already. Please.

Humidity wrapped around her and she tried to pull the warm soup into her lungs, but she couldn't seem to manage. Short breaths didn't allow enough oxygen in and she leaned against a lamppost, desperate to slow everything down or risk suffocation. Deep trembling in her muscles threatened to bring her to her knees.

People flowed around her, shooting her curious looks from under crinkled brows, but not slowing.

Taking careful steps, she walked across the brick of the sidewalk and shouldered through the glass door of a drugstore. The chill of the AC flowed over her skin and she closed her eyes for a moment. Cool air leaked into her lungs before finally easing into a steady flow.

On legs still shaking, she walked to the back of the store to grab a bottle of cola from the refrigerator and rolled it across her brow after paying.

Now what?

She had no idea what to do. Doctor? Shrink? A fucking exorcist?

The tavern already freaked her out, even more so in light of her new information, but it didn't bother her nearly as much as these … hallucinations. Were they really figments of a teetering mind? Wait. Didn't questioning it mean she wasn't insane? She'd never been clear on that.

Rowan pressed a hand to her forehead. Perhaps this whole adventure was a mistake. She could have sold the tavern and stayed in her little apartment in Toluca Lake to figure the next move.

But after Craig, she was so done with L.A. Following her heart had let to blind stupidity. The Galloping Goose had offered her a fresh start.

Yeah, a nice smooth sail into a padded room. If she returned home, her parents might even foot the bill.

She peered outside, fixing her gaze on individuals and groups as a whole, but the brilliant late-afternoon sun betrayed nothing ominous.

Unwilling to box herself into a cab or another streetcar, Rowan took a deep breath and stepped back outside for the walk home.

****

Rowan arrived back at the Goose from her bi-weekly excursion and didn't spare him a single glance. She walked right past and disappeared into the back hallway, her hands clenched at her sides.

He finished pulling a draft and set it before his customer, new urgency drawing up from low in his belly. Luke deliberated, stepped away from the bar and his responsibilities, decided 'screw it', and jerked his head at Christy when she buzzed by. "I'll be back. Hold the fort."

"Sure. Can do."

He slid from behind the bar, his strides long to eat up distance but not to appear hurried. He passed the darkened office and pushed into the stairwell, wondering if she'd even let him into the apartment.

No worries there.

Gazing upward, Luke stopped to lean against the balustrade. He shoved his hands in his pockets.

Rowan sat at the top of the steps, sunglasses now hanging on the front of her V-neck. She'd been staring into nothing and now, with apparent difficulty, shifted her gaze to him. "Don't you have a job to do?"

"Yeah and you're currently keeping me from it."

She met his eyes and it occurred to him she hadn't done so since he'd kissed her. The memory of it brought warmth to his insides but he kept his expression blank.

"Luke, after closing, I'd like to talk to you. I think I might need some … help. I mean, if you're okay with it."

He opened his mouth to respond with something caustic, but the profound sadness that seemed to emanate from her cut off the defensive impulse. "Is everything okay?"

Rowan stared down at him, her beautiful face

pinched and pale. "I think I might be going crazy, that's all."

His heart twisted in his chest and a low panic buzzed in his blood, but he kept his expression neutral. "I guess that merits discussion."

Turning, he pulled the door open to step back into the hallway.

"Luke?"

Hesitating, he shifted back to face her.

"Why did you kiss me?" Instead of curious, her voice sounded tired. Her gaze stuck to his face, wary but exhausted. "I thought you didn't like me. Hell, I thought you resented me."

Luke weighed his answer, contemplating the discussion he'd had earlier in the week with his deceased wife. He remembered Henry's somber comment. *The rest of your life is a long time to mourn.* It was so unbelievably difficult to move on. "You thought wrong."

He let the door swing shut behind him before she could witness emotions pushing out his threadbare control.

Chapter Fourteen

Rowan sat in the corner booth, hands clasping one another, jaw pulsing. Her hair hung loose past her shoulders, falling in tumbles of dark-cherry waves. She'd pushed it behind her ears and the glint of tiny pieces of jade graced the lobes.

Without bothering to ask, Luke grabbed a bottle of bourbon and two short glasses from behind the bar and crossed the dining room. He swung into the seat opposite her and poured each of them a double.

He waited.

Rowan glanced at him before studying the amber liquid in the glass.

"You look like you could use one."

Her lip twitched, but there was nothing humorous behind it. She reached to cradle the glass between her hands. "Thanks."

Luke watched her take a sip, noting the slight tremble of her hands.

"You live here all your life, Luke?" She shook her head. "Sorry. An assumption on my part. The accent I guess."

"Most of it." With the couple exceptions of college and a summer abroad. He took a swallow of his own drink, enjoying the smooth burn.

"You seem right at home with … Mavis, Robert, and whatever, whoever, else has decided to claim this place as their own. I'm wondering if that's the norm around here."

"Seems like you've accepted them."

"Always thought I had an open mind, but when it came to the supernatural, well, that's always been a tough one." She shrugged and allowed a tiny laugh. "Not anymore, though. I guess it's probably because my parents are … the way they are. My dad's a doctor, a plastic surgeon, and my mom, well, she's big on the hospital fundraising scene. They're not people to encourage flights of fancy or anything. I know that sounds weird since my dad, in his way, sells fantasy, but it's a business. They're actually both pragmatic to a fault. That's why they were so pissed off when I left college to try my hand at acting. Especially my mom." Rowan took another swallow of bourbon. "Now I'm making them sound bad and that's not my intention. They're decent people. Just not … prone to believing a lot of things."

"It's hard to believe what hasn't been experienced," Luke murmured, a little surprised at her admission. She went out of her way to avoid talking about herself. Of course, he was just as guilty. "There's much more out there than people see or want to see."

Leaning back, he waited, instinctively knowing the crux of the discussion was coming up.

She pressed the heel of her hand to her forehead and squeezed her eyes shut. Several long moments later, she took another drink and locked her gaze on his. "Tell me about my uncle."

Frowning, he tilted his head. "What about him?"

"You said you weren't aware of any gambling or anything like that. To be honest, I'm not sure I believe you. You were his friend, so it's reasonable to assume you'd only protect him. What I want to know is if he acted … differently … before his death." Rowan finished her drink, and although her movements had turned a little sluggish, her gray eyes were direct. He wondered for how much longer.

"In what way?"

"You tell me."

"What happened today?" He topped off their

drinks, pushed the bottle aside. "Are you in trouble?"

"Don't turn this around on me. Please. I need to know if Jimmy seemed scared, maybe even paranoid. Was he afraid to leave the bar?"

Guilt cut into his insides and he couldn't say a word for several long moments. Rowan continued to stare at him, waiting. But he was relieved to find no accusation in her eyes.

"There was something going on, but he wouldn't talk to me," Luke conceded and shoved a hand through his hair. "He seemed distracted, not himself. Pisses me off because maybe I could have helped."

"He didn't trust you? That seems unlikely … considering."

Insult flared but blew itself out. "No, that wasn't it. If anything, I think he was … ashamed."

Fear glazed her eyes but her face remained stoic. "Huh."

She squeezed the drink between her hands and he had the faintest vision of it cracking and exploding. "You found him, didn't you? It wasn't a heart attack, then?"

"Sure it was." He finished his whiskey and returned it to the tabletop with a thud. "But isn't that anyone's cause of death? Heart stops, life stops."

Swallowing, she dropped her gaze to the glass cradled in her palms, seemed to debate before finishing it. "Don't play with me. There's more. I can tell there's more."

"All right, there's more." He leaned close, forearms braced, hands fisted. Temper, grief, and a healthy dose of fear for this woman twisted him up inside. "Usually a heart attack doesn't make a man punch holes in walls, throw things, smash his hand through a pane of glass, or turn his hair white."

Eyes widening, she opened her mouth and shut it

again. A thin sheen of sweat touched her forehead and Luke felt sick inside. "The authorities…"

"See what they want to see. Locked door from the inside. A man who'd grown really eccentric pops off, goes over. They think loose wiring in his head because the autopsy is what it is. He suffered from Paget's, which is some kind of bone thing, but the official cause of death was basically a clot in the heart. No drugs that they could detect, no defensive wounds, nothing to indicate anyone was there but him."

"Weren't you downstairs?" she whispered.

Luke shook his head with a grim smile. "That was the weekend I decided to visit my mother in Shreveport. Got back early Monday morning."

Rowan curled forward to stare dully at the distressed wood of the table, even as he stared at her. "What did he see that night?"

Luke said nothing, knowing the softly uttered question wasn't directed at him. His own imagination had gone dark and depraved when he'd asked himself the same damned thing. Taking an extra moment, he refilled their glasses.

Finally, she looked up. "You said that you could have helped him? How?"

"I said maybe." Luke hesitated before pushing on. "I can't help but wonder if he got himself involved with a bokor."

Her eyes widened. "What's a bokor?"

"Open mind, remember?"

Rowan nodded, a frown crinkling her brow. She sipped her drink, and sipped again. Finished.

"There are some very superstitious people in this area who believe in the power of voodoo. I'm sure that's not news to you. I mean, it is New Orleans. Most of it's pretty harmless. Touristy crap. Love, luck, libido, that kind of thing. But not all of it. A bokor is kind of a witch doctor who deals in spells, but where most priests or priestesses use white magic, a bokor does whatever he needs to do to get any job done."

"Whatever it takes…" she murmured, gazing at him, darkness in her eyes. "What does that mean?"

"It means he'll use white magic or black magic. They're known to mess with some pretty dark forces."

"And you believe this?" Her hand shook when she refilled her glass.

Luke sighed, long and heavy. "My logical side says no. I mean, I went to college and thought I moved beyond superstition, but growing up here, you see things, hear things. And they don't always have a solid explanation."

"The ghosts for instance." A smile twitched at her lips but didn't quite form.

"I guess so."

"This guy who's … harassing me … or maybe he's technically haunting me, I don't know, but he says Jimmy left a debt and he expects me to pick up the tab."

"That's why you were asking about gambling…" Luke sat back to search his memory before snapping back at her words. "What did you say? Has someone actually threatened you?"

They both jumped when a frigid wind blew through the tavern, rattling glasses and making the lights flicker. A moment later, the jukebox came alive with Screamin' Jay Hawkins singing about putting a spell on someone. Luke glanced around, clenching his jaw in annoyance, figuring one of the ghosts had discovered a new talent.

It cut off seconds later, leaving a long silence broken only by the occasional rumble of traffic.

  ****

Rowan took a breath and let it out in a slow trickle, but it did nothing to ease the sound of her heart blaring in her ears. "Um, that was unexpected."

"Has someone been threatening you?" He came back to the point without comment.

"Yes, I think. But not exactly."

"What does that even mean?" he demanded.

His tone managed to elicit a spark of aggravation within her and she narrowed her eyes.

"It means I have no proof. Half the time I can't even quite remember what he looks like afterward. And before you get you boxers in a twist, I'm not looking for a protector. I can take care of myself. I'd just like to have an idea what I'm up against."

"Accepting ghosts is one thing. But if this is a bokor, you're in way over your head."

"And what are you … thinking?" Dizziness swooped in and she pressed her fingers to her temple. "Hell, I think I'm going to sell this place and go home."

Luke didn't answer and when she looked up, his expression held something too close to sympathy. Her anxiety and fear ratcheted up into the stratosphere.

"What? Why are you looking at me like that?" Panic raced up her spine.

He leaned forward and she caught a subtle whiff of his aftershave. "It won't matter where you are."

His voice had gone so gentle. It was a tone she'd never heard from him and nothing could have frightened her more. Rowan pushed up against the table. "Am I destined for white hair and a heart attack at twenty-eight? Is that what you're saying?"

She climbed to her feet, swaying. The vulnerability of intoxication brought back the sting of tears and her vision blurred. "Am I dead because of something my uncle did? Something he got mixed up in?"

Luke shook his head and stepped toward her. "No, we can try to fix this."

"How? You haven't seen him. He's solid, then he's a shadow. Then your brain goes to mush and your muscles freeze. I can take care of myself, I swear I can. Someone tried to mug me in Hollywood once and I kicked his balls into oatmeal. But this is something ... different."

He winced and cleared his throat. "I know someone who can help. At least, I used to."

"Is it a curse? Am I cursed?" She turned, stumbled, but he caught her arm to keep her upright. "I need to ... go." Where did she need to go? Where could she? She had no idea, but the persistent urge to escape turned all encompassing.

"You need to get some sleep and prepare for a wicked hangover. We'll take care of this. You're not going to drop over dead at the age of twenty-eight." Luke ran his hand over her hair and she frowned.

Shaking her head, Rowan tried to pull away when the room tilted. "Shit. I think I'm going to fall..."

"I've got you."

****

Rowan rolled over, cracked her eyes open, and wished she hadn't. Lightning bolts of pain zapped the inside of her brain and ricocheted around to further the damage.

This was why she didn't drink that often.

Blinking several times, she squinted in confusion at her bedside table. A bottle of water and a smaller one of aspirin stood within easy reach.

The flush of embarrassment hit her and heat crept over her skin with happy little feet. Her memory was harsh, unwavering.

Shit. Why couldn't she be one of those fools who forgot everything after a bout with liquor?

Luke had carried her upstairs when the room wouldn't stop spinning. Carried. Her. Upstairs. Some ultra-primitive part of her acknowledged how his arms had felt solid, safe around her, even as the modern part tried to drop-kick it out of her brain.

Embarrassment spiked into humiliation when she caught the whiff of coffee from the front room. Oh, God. He was still here. Had she slept with him? And here she thought she'd remembered everything. In a swift move that made her brain sing horribly off-note, she flipped off the comforter, relief a cool blanket across her flesh.

With the exception of her shoes, she was fully dressed.

Squeezing her eyes shut, she rubbed her forehead. Agitation and headache warred within the confines of her skull. Taking a moment to pop a couple of aspirins, she washed them down before following her nose to the siren-scent of caffeine.

Luke was slumped on the couch, long legs stretched out over the coffee table, crossed at the ankles. The morning television news yammered from talking heads opposite him. His hair was mussed into spikes, face coated with morning beard growth. The first word that settled into her hangover-infused mind was 'sexy' and she gritted her teeth against it. "You didn't have to stay, you know."

He stared at her, those dark-blue eyes cool on hers. "You have a TV."

"I'm glad you have your priorities." She poured a cup of coffee, almost purring over the aroma. Rowan peered beyond the steam at him. "Thank you."

"Welcome."

"This is awkward."

"Not for me."

She scowled and sipped her coffee, the boost initially psychological. The physical would be along in short order.

He tilted his head and studied her, a faint smile holding around his eyes. "Only bar owner I've ever met that can't hold their booze."

Leaning against the counter, she glowered at him. "In fairness, I've only been a bar owner a couple of months. Maybe I'll build up a tolerance." She took another sip, the warmth struggling to push out the sudden cold when her thoughts turned. "If I live that long."

Luke stared at her for a long moment, pressing his lips together. Glancing at his watch, he nodded. "We have time to take a side trip this morning. It's been a few years, and I've kind of lost touch, but with any luck, she's still alive and in the area."

"That's not very heartening."

"Hell, this woman will probably outlive us all." The dark-blue of his eyes shifted into uncertainty, almost embarrassment. "I remember my grandmother and Mrs. Leroux talking about local voodoo shops, I mean the real deal. I also remember her just … knowing things. Like she could peel away all my layers and see what I was thinking." A smile shoved at his discomfort. "Pretty disconcerting for a kid, I'll tell you that."

"I bet," she murmured, gazing at him over the rim of her mug. She was unsure what to think about any of this but fascinated at the change she saw in him.

"Last time I saw her, she still made me feel the same damned way." He shook his head, what appeared to be sadness flitting through his eyes. The moment then broke and he raised his brows. "You want the bathroom first?"

Mind wandering, Rowan shook her head and took another sip of coffee. "Help yourself."

Chapter Fifteen

"You're kidding." They'd made the short hike to the storage facility and she now looked at him, wary. He wasn't sure what she'd expected, but the huge Harley evidently wasn't it.

"You've never ridden on a bike? A big city girl like you?" Luke didn't bother to hide his amusement. "This is the fastest choice. Of course, I could see about a rental car or a cab. Or you could break down and buy a car. Your call."

She hesitated, but the wariness turned cool at his not-so-subtle taunts.

He rubbed his brow and shook his head. "I understand if you don't trust me, but think about this: I don't want to die any more than you do." He pushed out a side smirk. "Besides, it's a hell of a rush."

She narrowed her eyes before setting her jaw. "Fine. Let's go."

"Good choice." He rolled the bike from the metal enclosure before pulling out his barely-used helmet and shoving it over her head. Taking a moment, he paused to adjust the chin strap. "A little big, but better than nothing. Get on and hold tight."

He looped one leg over the big motorcycle and looked at her, waiting.

Following suit, she climbed on behind him, lightly resting her hands against his ribcage. When he revved the bike and started to roll, she grabbed hold, arms wrapped around his midsection tightly.

"Relax. It'll be fine!" He called over the engine, before leaning into the turn and heading toward the freeway.

Luke was glad she couldn't see his face.

Despite the circumstances, the feel of her molding herself against him brought about a little high, a little reminder that he was still alive and puttering around this insane world. Darkness wasn't as complete as he'd once believed.

Now he needed to make sure it stayed that way.

He guided the big bike away from the city, heading west on the interstate, enjoying the ride, trying to push the situation to the back of his mind. There'd be enough time to pull it back out for scrutiny. The prospect scraped his insides raw.

It wasn't far, but it may as well have been. So much had changed since he'd attended his grand-mere's funeral all those years ago. Then he'd still been a husband and father, at least for a few months longer, not the breathing corpse he'd become.

For a fraction of a second, anger surged to a knife point and he almost pushed the bike faster. Rowan's grip on him tempered the impulse. Her fingers twisted into the cotton of his t-shirt with a strength and ferocity that described the woman perfectly. Or it could have been panic too.

Luke grinned at the thought.

"How much farther?" Her voice whipped out at him and it held no fear. He figured she had to be hiding it. Pride wasn't just vanity with this one.

"Not much."

A few minutes later, he left the interstate to merge onto a local highway south, reducing his speed to a crawl. Today wasn't the day to get pulled over by small-town law enforcement.

Luke shot a glance upward in speculation. The azure skies above them were getting shoved out by thickening gray clouds. He loved riding the bike, but riding in the rain kind of sucked.

Too late to worry about it now.

The town hadn't changed, freezing in time as some rare places did. He didn't know if it was comforting or depressing. They passed the old high school, the painting of the mascot on the side of the gym still dull and faded. Several restaurants he'd been subjected to as a kid lined the main street, punctuated with a few he actually enjoyed.

"Did you grow up here?"

Luke slid a glance over his shoulder, a sense of warm recollection settling over him. "Yes and no. I spent my summers here with my grandmother."

He nodded to a strip mall on their left. A tiny bakery/coffee shop capped the end, nestled next to a drycleaners. "The first place I got fired from when I was sixteen."

"What did you do?"

"I didn't hear an order right. When the customer asked if I was stupid, I bounced an apple fritter off his forehead."

"Well, I guess that would do it."

His laugh rang out and he was only marginally surprised to find it genuine.

****

A few minutes later, Luke leaned into a right turn as homes replaced businesses. The lots were large, houses small but well maintained. He slowed past a cute brick traditional with a long driveway and birdbath. Rowan thought for a moment that he was rolling to a stop, but he kept going for another half-block before turning again.

He pulled up to the curb before a small, clapboard bungalow. The home was painted a pale peach with white framing two large pictures windows in front. A driveway leading into a carport stood adjacent, next to a well-manicured front yard. A middle-age woman in a broad hat, a tank top, and capris tended flowers on either side of the front stoop. She stopped to twist and gaze at them.

"What can I do for you?" She smiled and grabbed the brim of her hat when a sudden strong breeze tried to whisk it away.

"We were actually looking for Ruth Leroux." Luke strode forward and Rowan kept pace, pulling off the helmet and letting it dangle at her side.

"Well…" The woman's forehead creased in thought. "I don't know about a Ruth, but I bought this place a couple years back from a David Leroux. Maybe he might have been kin?"

"Yeah, that's her son. Do you happen to still have his contact information? I hate to bother you, ma'am, but you see, Mrs. Leroux and my grand-mere were good friends. When I was a kid, I used to sit in that little kitchen in there, eating cookies and listening to them yap." He jerked his chin toward the house.

"So, you were in town and decided to take a chance?"

"Yes, ma'am." Luke allowed a brilliant smile and Rowan stared at him.

"Well, let me see what I can find. Why don't you both come in for some iced tea? It may take a few minutes."

"Thank you, Miss…?"

The woman blushed "Mrs. Tulley. Rebekah Tulley."

"Very nice to meet you Mrs. Tulley. My name's Luke Meunier and this is Rowan O'Herley." He walked up the path and Rowan followed, still gaping at him.

If he didn't lower the charm wattage, the woman might attack him, husband or no husband. It appeared her surly bartender had gone into temporary hiding today and Rowan still felt a little blindsided.

She stepped over the threshold into a comfortable little living area with polished wood floors, a cream-colored sofa, and the pop of a red viscose area rug beneath. High ceilings, crown molding, and recessed lighting above gave the room the illusion of more space.

"You have a beautiful home, Mrs. Tulley."

"Why, thank you, sweetie! I love fiddling around with design." She disappeared into the next room. "This way!"

Luke raised his brows and gave her a long look.

"What? You're not the only one who can be pleasant and cordial if need be," Rowan muttered, scowling.

He shrugged and paused to wave her before him.
****

"It's odd that she invited two complete strangers into her home and not only that, she served them tea and coffee cake, too." Rowan shook her head in wonder.

"Small towns. It's a dying way of life." He pulled out his phone and plugged in the number he'd been given, hoping it was current. With a mixture of relief and annoyance, he was forced to leave a message for David Leroux before shoving the cell back into his pocket. "Let's hope he gets back or I might have to look to other avenues."

He went to swing his leg over the bike before realizing Rowan had stopped.

She'd gone still, staring at nothing, expression empty. Luke acted on pure instinct. Deferring to his heart, he wrapped his arms around her to pull her close, brushing a kiss to her temple. "Trust me. We'll take care of this."

She didn't move, arms hanging at her sides. "You

know, for a bit there, I'd forgotten. And now, as I think about it, I don't want to accept it, acknowledge it. Not in the brightness of the day. It should be a bad dream, unnerving but easy to move beyond. But not this time. He appeared to me during the day, more than once." Rowan looked up at him, gaze roaming around his face. "Makes it easier to think I'm just nuts."

He ran his hands up and down her arms, his touch gentle. "You're not nuts."

"How could you even know that?"

Luke said nothing, but his face hardened.

"And I still don't understand you. Why are you even bothering with this? What's in it for you, other than a major headache?"

Unable to give her any kind of real answer, Luke glanced up when a light spray of rain flicked against him. "Let's go grab some real breakfast. Maybe Leroux will touch base by that time and we'll go from there."

He handed her the helmet, and after a moment, she obliged him by putting it on.

****

It was a casual place, built out of an old two-story house with plantation shutters. Cement floors and seating with brightly colored plastic tablecloths contrasted with sunny yellow walls, but Rowan didn't seem to pay attention.

Luke showed her to a corner table by the window and shoved a menu in her hand. "Order something and eat before you disappear."

"You're not my keeper."

"No, but if I'm going to the trouble to try to help you out, you could at least not starve yourself."

She stared at him, the lovely deep smoky mist of her eyes meeting his. Those odd dark flecks shot through them like lightning. A little tremor shook his insides, but

117

he didn't break the contact. "You didn't answer my question. Are you doing this because you feel you owe my uncle some kind of allegiance? Or is it something else?"

The server came by and Luke ordered two breakfast po'boys, a side of praline bacon, orange juice, and coffee. On short but quick legs, the woman swept off with a nod and a smile, and Rowan curled a lip. "Is this your plan? I get fat and drop over from a heart attack before he has a chance to do it for me?"

"I get the feeling you'll burn it off in angry energy alone."

She glared at him before offering the smallest of shrugs. "Probably. Not one of my most sterling traits. My temper, I mean."

Leaning back, Luke considered her. "I know I'm somewhat to blame."

"You give yourself too much credit."

The waitress dropped off their drinks and Rowan smiled in gratitude, grabbing the coffee with barely disguised relief.

"So, I don't piss you off?" His lips twitched.

"Of course you piss me off. You're not the first either and I doubt you'll be the last. According to my folks, I was born with a hair trigger. I have gotten better though."

"I would never have called that."

When she glowered at him, he widened his eyes, midnight-blue glinting in tease. "What did I say?"

"You're purposely distracting me."

"Maybe."

****

The server came by a few minutes later with breakfast, and despite herself, Rowan's stomach shrieked with anger and then glee. The heady aroma drifted up, catching her off guard.

"No, but this will. Take my word for it." He grabbed a piece of bacon first and ripped into it before picking up his breakfast sandwich.

She analyzed what sat before her and couldn't keep herself from digging in. Her taste buds did a happy dance, and she took another bite. She'd only be able to eat half of the huge sandwich, but what a lovely half it would have been.

"What about you? You have any sibs?" Rowan wiped her mouth and turned an inquisitive eye on the man across from her.

"Half-sister. Older. Lives in Ohio." He took another bite and offered nothing more.

"Well, as always, you're just so forthcoming with information." A hesitant smile played around her lips, but her breath hitched for the smallest second. Her curiosity gnawed at her, but she couldn't bring herself to ask the big questions. She doubted he'd even answer.

"I can guess what you'd really like to know." As if reading her mind, his voice lowered into a murmur, gaze finding hers, holding, letting go.

"It's none of my business." Uncertainty laced her words, but she tamped down the compassion burgeoning inside.

Luke continued to eat, but tension settled around his eyes in the same moment he appeared to retreat to a distant time. His jaw throbbed a moment later and he shook his head as if dismissing the subject.

She shoved back her own fears and instinctively reached out to touch his hand. "I'm sorry for what you went through. Whatever it may have been."

He slowly turned his hand palm up. After the slightest hesitation, she settled hers against it and his fingers curled around her. His skin was rough, a little calloused. Working man's hands. Large and warm. Energy sizzled into her flesh, and Rowan held her breath, pulling her fixated stare from their entwined hands, up to his eyes.

A deep, rich-blue gaze met hers, holding, burning with such intensity she couldn't pull in her next breath, nor look away.

When the phone rang, they both startled. He tugged his hand from hers, face hardening. She dropped her gaze, pulled in that reluctant breath and let it out in a whoosh, face hot, mind fragmented.

Rowan was dimly aware of him speaking, but didn't absorb his words. She narrowed her gaze beyond him, out the window, into the light. People wandered past, intent on their day and wherever it would take them. She half-expected to see the green-eyed man. When she didn't, she half-wondered if she was making something out of nothing.

Luke's one-word acknowledgements and answers bounced off of her, her concentration loopy and wavering. She continued to watch foot traffic. So many different ages, shapes, and sizes, most hurrying, some idle. Her melancholy stayed with her, a blur of gray on her periphery.

The sudden grip on her arm had her gasping and pulling to free herself.

"Stop it. It's just me." Luke muttered, his voice bordering on a low growl.

Rowan blinked, feeling an uneasy twist of embarrassment and annoyance. Her irritation fled at the sudden white pallor of his face.

"What's wrong?"

"That was Andy."

Her brain reached and grabbed at new faces and names, settling on one in particular. "What's happened?"

"Henry. We … I have to go. I can drop you off at The Goose if you want, but I need to get to the hospital."

Fear for the sweet little man made her throat dry and all thoughts of her boogeyman flitted from her brain. "No need. I'll go with you."

Chapter Sixteen

Rain had heightened from drizzle to brisk drops, but it didn't keep Luke from making good time. He found a space in the parking garage and broke into a run, with Rowan keeping up with minimal effort.

Luke stomped past the information desk, heading toward the elevators without pause. There was no hesitation, no sense of confusion normally indicative of a hospital visit. He knew exactly where he was going and Rowan wondered how often he'd been inside the cavernous building. A raw feeling of melancholy scraped her insides when the answer occurred to her.

He said little, but his body hummed with stress. When she couldn't stand it any longer, she reached for his hand. To her surprise, he allowed it for a short moment before pulling away when the elevator doors opened. He made a quick left, stepping through the hushed hallway, past a nurse's station before finding Andy outside room 306.

Rowan hung back, uncomfortable with intruding, wondering if she should have had Luke drop her off at the tavern.

The two men shook hands as Andy raised his brows at Rowan. A strained smile lit his face. "Ms. O'Herley. My father would be pleased you came."

"Rowan."

He nodded, worried gaze leaving her and fixing on Luke. "I found him this morning. They say he had a stroke. He's conscious, but not completely lucid. Kind of goes in and out." He ran a shaking hand down his face. "Jenny's visiting her mother in Baton Rouge, but she's on her way home now. So are the girls. College kids get so busy, but they adore their papa. I know you're pretty close with him, too, so I figured you might want to know. Hope I didn't catch you at a bad time. I called some of his other friends too … shit, I'm babbling…"

"No, no. I wasn't far. I'm glad you contacted me." Luke peered past him through the glass walls to the figure swallowed by machines. "Jesus."

"They're only letting one person in at a time." Andy gazed at his father as well. "It's bad when they lose consciousness. He was out when I found him. They're pumping him full of all kinds of drugs and there might be some other kind of procedure, but…oh hell, I don't even know…"

When he tapered off, Luke squeezed his shoulder.

"I'll go get you some coffee, Andy. You look like you could use some." Rowan offered, the urge to do something, anything, rattling around inside.

He blinked at her. "Oh. That would be nice. Thank you."

Rowan caught Luke's gaze and jerked her head to the side. "We passed an alcove down the hall with vending machines. I'll be right back."

She slipped back the way they'd come, mind spinning around the morning's events. When it settled, it landed on Henry with a hollow thump. She pictured him in her head, the crinkled face, the broad smile, how he'd endeavored to teach her to jitterbug. How he'd purposely goaded Luke into dancing with her, much to their respective annoyance.

The vending area was off the staircase, and Rowan stepped inside, reaching in her purse for change. A parade of snacks and drinks vied for her attention and she wondered when Andy had eaten last. Maybe a candy bar or something would be good. But what if he was diabetic? She didn't know anything about him.

Prickles on the nape of her neck had her pivoting,

and she pressed her back into the corner, gaze sweeping ahead. From her position, she could see the heavy door to the stairs and the far-left elevator. The hum of its ascent reached her ears, as the long push bar across the stairwell entryway rattled.

Every muscle in her body locked, including her lungs. They allowed no movement and all Rowan could do was stare, helpless in panic, but recognizing the burn of anger underneath.

Hadn't she wanted him to show himself just the other day? She'd been armed with her ridiculous pepper spray, ready to do battle against her boogeyman. When he did appear, she'd cut and run. In retrospect, canned cayenne was probably pretty damned ineffective on spirit stalkers, or whatever the hell he was. She'd been lucky she hadn't inadvertently sprayed a senior citizen in her panic.

With effort, she pulled in a partial breath, eyes fixed before her. She vaguely wondered if they'd find her passed out against machines offering stale snacks and abysmal coffee. Never before in her life had she been subject to panic attacks. It gave her new sympathy for those plagued by them.

Another small breath, another small victory.

The stairwell door flew open at the same time the elevator stopped at the floor with a loud ping. A family converged before her, a boy about twelve razzing a girl a few years younger with, "I beat you! I told you the stairs are faster!" while their mother rushed to hush them both.

Feeling foolish, Rowan sucked in a huge scorching breath and took a moment to steady herself. Low burning temper had her contemplating kicking the wall, but wisdom intervened. She didn't need any broken toes.

She paid for Andy's coffee and returned to room

306.

Andy stood outside the window, looking in. His reflection projected a beaten man, hands shoved deep in his pockets, face long and haggard. Rowan would have pegged him for mid- to late-forties, but worry for his father lumped an easy twenty years on him. He accepted the hot drink with a small smile. "Thanks. That was sweet of you."

She nodded, stood next to him, and gazed through the glass.

"I suppose I'm not used to my father being so helpless. I know he's not a big man … physically, but to me, he always seemed so large and full of life." Andy smiled and shook his head. "He has a way of manipulating you to think his ideas are actually your ideas. Used to piss me off so much when I was younger. Still does sometimes, but most of time, his thoughts have a lot of merit."

"I know Luke respects him immensely."

The man made a little acknowledging sound in his throat and took a sip of coffee.

Luke had pulled up the one lonely chair and sat holding his old friend's hand. His lips moved, but the words would never penetrate beyond them. They were meant for Henry and Henry alone. Something warm and unexpected glowed deep inside Rowan at the honest affection she witnessed and she had to look away to keep the tickle in her nose from erupting into glazing tears.

"Luke is a good man, ma chère. I know he can be…" Andy shook his head, a low chuckle escaping. "As asshole sometimes, but tragedy has a way of leaving a mark. Not everyone comes back, you know?"

"No, they don't." Her heart thrummed.

"He shut too many people out, so they gave up, went on. But you know how that goes. A few of us hung in, because we remember who he is and what he's capable of."

"And what's that?" she whispered.

"The type of man who'd give his life for those he cares about. And he almost did." Andy turned and studied her for a moment before his eyes retreated and his skin flushed. "You don't know. I'm sorry … I just assumed because you're both here…"

"It's not like that." She wasn't exactly sure what it was, though, at least not anymore. Things had become much more complex than she'd bargained for.

"I see. Well, you'll forgive me if I leave it at that. Luke will talk to you, or he won't, but it's up to him. I guess I started babbling again. Pardon … I'm sorry."

"I understand." Rowan reached out and squeezed the man's arm. "Anyway, this isn't about Luke or me. This is about Henry. We're here for him."

"Yes. Thank you. I appreciate that."

Inside the room, Luke leaned forward to listen as the old man spoke. He nodded, a grim smile turning the corners of his mouth up. Gently, Luke released Henry's hand, got up, and kissed him on the forehead. The tenderness of the gesture overwhelmed her and despite her struggle, a tear escaped and rolled down Rowan's cheek. She swept it away and turned when Luke walked out.

Before she could say anything, the sound of footsteps filled the hall and a plump woman with a pretty face enfolded Andy in her arms, murmuring to him in French.

"I think it's time for us to go. Henry's grandkids will be here soon." Luke angled his head and Rowan fell into step with him as they headed for the elevators.

****

"Well, hell."

The rain came down in opaque sheets, flooding the streets and sidewalks and peaking the humidity into triple digits. It coated her skin with a sticky film and the idea of riding in the rain actually held some appeal. "We're not all that far, right?"

"Not really." He cocked his head. "We could always call a cab for you."

"What the hell for?"

A smile twitched his lips, but his eyes remained somber. "Okay, your call."

Luke mounted the bike and waited while she did likewise. Rowan wrapped her arms around him and hesitated before resting her cheek to his back. She could hear his steady heartbeat and the whoosh of his breath, and for some reason, she took comfort from it.

Despite the deluge, he took his time, remaining vigilant. When they finally returned the bike to storage and made the trek home, they were soaked through their clothing. Despite the heaviness of the air, the rain felt cool against her skin.

Rowan stopped to tilt her head upward, enjoying the flow over her face and throat.

"Don't turkeys drown that way?"

"Good thing I'm not a turkey."

This time he did smile, barely a smirk, but his worry seemed to retreat in the expression. He stared at her intently and heat burst in her cheeks.

"Stop that." She began walking again, pushing her hair back, feeling its weight against her shoulders. "You're creepy when you stare."

"Am I?" He strode beside her, slitting side glances down her way.

Rowan became a little too conscious of her clothing sticking to her and she plucked at her top in an attempt to compensate. Not that it did a lot of good. The rain had tapered off a bit but still remained steady. She was also a little too aware of that dark-blue gaze on her. In a rush, gooseflesh dotted her skin and she pressed her lips together, swearing internally.

They were a half-block from The Galloping Goose when he reached out to take her arm, his grasp firm but gentle. "Rowan."

He'd stopped, head down but peering up at her. His midnight eyes were troubled and an underlying tension simmered within. His body stiffened and he opened his mouth as if to say something before shutting it with a shake of his head.

"Is something—"

Before she realized it, he pulled her against him, framed her face and pressed his lips to hers. Swallowing her squeak of surprise, his hands glided down to secure around her waist when she opened to him, gentle and soft, building into passion. With little hesitation, she reached up and threaded her fingers into his wet hair, leaning into him, even as her logical side wondered what the hell she was doing.

Rain funneled down and around them and his hold tightened, molding her close, his mouth setting her on fire, sending ripples of heat through her flesh, through her loins. One hand snaked up to weave into her hair, tugging her head back for better access, the kiss hungrier, ravaging.

Her body shook, blood burning from the inside out. Rowan ran her hands across his shoulders, allowing one to caress his cheek, skin smooth and firm from his recent shave.

The world and rain dissolved around them until the distant sound of yelling snapped her back and away. With some hesitation, Luke let her go, watching as she hurried away.

****

A couple of teenagers standing under an overhang across the street hooted, clapped, and grinned. Both were carbon copies, hair flopping in their eyes and skateboards in hand.

"Don't you guys have school or something?" Luke called out, his voice rumbling with displeasure.

"Teacher in-service day, dude! Better catch her. She's trying to ditch ya!" They screamed with laughter when he turned to see Rowan steps from the tavern, pulling out her keys with shaking hands.

He caught up with her as she pulled the door open and slipped inside. His heart continued to race, heated passion still firing within its beats. "I'm sorry. I shouldn't have done that."

"Are you, really? Sorry, I mean."

Frowning, Luke gazed down at her, seeing the lovely flush settle across her cheeks. Soft gray eyes had shifted to coal, lips parted, light makeup smeared from his impulsive kiss and a rainy morning. He shook his head. "No, I guess I'm not."

"I don't know what to think of you. You're rude, abrasive, often condescending, but I don't think that's really you. I think it might be a smokescreen designed to scare people away." She stepped close and he held his breath. "I think you do it to protect yourself from caring too much, but guess what? Your armor is cracking. I can see it," she murmured, as if to herself.

"What did Andy say to you?"

"He made some assumptions, but when he realized I didn't know what the hell he was talking about, he clammed up." She reached up to trail her fingertips down his jawline. "You have good friends, Luke."

With a sigh, he leaned down to rest his forehead to hers and closed his eyes. "I don't want to care about you, Rowan." Or want her, but he did so much it burrowed into his soul.

He felt it, a whisper of her lips against his. "Then why do you?"

"I can't seem to help myself," he murmured in truth, losing himself to her for another moment before she pulled away with a gentle pat to his chest.

"Since we still have a business to run, I need to go change." She walked away from him and he watched her go, heart leaden but trembling. He'd gone ahead and fallen into the trap he'd sworn he'd never allow again.

Now he had little choice but to see things through, praying the fates wouldn't choose to rip his life apart a second time.

Chapter Seventeen

"You aren't an easy person to reach."

Rowan took a breath and cringed, wishing she'd forgotten to turn on her ringer. On top of everything else, this was the last thing she needed. "Hi, Mom. How are things?"

"Good, actually, although I have the feeling you're avoiding your dad and me."

In the background, she could hear the rise and fall of Vivaldi. Rowan imagined her mother sitting in the corner of the white leather sectional, gazing out the picture window at the perfectly landscaped back garden, sipping some Pinot and listening to Winter. Like retail, Mom was always one season ahead. Melancholy stole through Rowan as it always did, but the low burn of anger followed behind. After everything she'd experienced, her parents' world seemed all the more ridiculous and superficial.

"That's silly." She kept her thoughts from entering her voice and stopped in mid-stride on her way out the door. Christy's youngest son had spiked a fever early in the day, so Rowan needed to take her place. Friday nights were a bear and she couldn't leave Taylor and Zoe on their own, at least not in good conscience. Besides, she desperately needed to stay busy. It was the only way to block out the insanity. "It's been kind of crazy getting everything organized."

"Did he leave a mess for you to sort through, sweetheart?"

"No, not really. The place has a solid foundation, solid customers. I think it just needs a little TLC." She dropped onto Jimmy's battered but comfy, old couch, surprised when her enthusiasm surged upward. "I have lots of ideas for a bit of a facelift, but also to bring in more customers."

"That's wonderful. You were always so creative. I can only imagine what you could do if you'd finished school."

Rowan's enthusiasm withered. "I'm doing all right."

"Oh, I'm sure you are. I was only saying—"

"I know what you were saying," She swallowed a sigh, pinched the bridge of her nose, and threw out a bone. "Maybe I'll even go back when things calm down. LSU is a good school."

There was a long pause on the other end. She was probably helping herself to a second glass of wine. "That would be lovely, Rowan."

As nice as the words were, the stilted tone said a little more. LSU wasn't Stanford. Rowan ignored it. "Anyway, how's Dad? Any new and interesting patients?"

The simple question sent Patricia Broussard O'Herley into a session of who's who in the wonderful world of plastic surgery. Rowan didn't really listen, biding her time, and jumping in when her mother paused for a breath. "I'm sorry, Mom, I really need to go. It's Friday night, so you can imagine how busy it's going to be."

"I know bars can get kind of rowdy on the weekends. I hope you're watching out for yourself." It must have been the tail end of Winter because Andrea Bocelli now replaced Vivaldi.

Rowan gritted her teeth. "It's not that kind of place, Mom. We've got some great people who come in here."

"Speaking of people, is that Meunier man still there? God, I hope not. I understand your uncle was helping him out—Jimmy was always a little foolish in that department, but I presume the man has moved on by now."

Stilling, Rowan grasped the phone a little tighter, loosening her hold when her fingers cramped. "Jimmy mentioned Luke Meunier to you?"

"During one of his more lucid moments. The situation was tragic, losing his wife and daughter that way, but he couldn't continue to live in that bar. That's not much of a life for anyone. People like that can sometimes get a little too comfortable and I wouldn't want him to take advantage of you."

"Of course not." Rowan's throat and mouth felt parched as her breath whooshed in and out, dry as sand. Her heart thumped in her temple and she rubbed it with her fingertips. "Um, I'll talk to you later, Mom. Give my love to Dad."

Nauseated, she disconnected.
****

Rowan moved as fast as she could, gaining a quick admiration for food servers. On a customer's suggestion, she'd arranged for another local band and the crowd they brought in hummed with energy and appetite. She was too busy to think about current events, let alone worry over them. Everything felt normal, real, tangible, and the whole idea of voodoo slid into the ridiculous.

As she flitted between table, kitchen, and bar, she could feel the sultry weight of Luke's gaze and tried not to react. Knowing a little about his past brought heaviness to her heart, but it still couldn't keep the tingle from lighting her blood. Torn, she tried to balance her attraction and her compassion. When it didn't work, she concentrated on the job.

During one of Rowan's loops, Margie hooked an arm though hers and Rowan smiled at her. "You're turning into one of my best customers. Was that the case when Jimmy owned the bar?"

The woman grinned back, speaking loudly over the background chaos. "Well, you do bring in some great entertainment. I think he was content to leave it as your local, neighborhood watering hole without a lot of hoopla." Her smile dimmed a little. "I wanted to ask how everything was going, I mean, personally. The last time I saw you, you seemed a little upset."

At the concern in the woman's dark eyes, Rowan considered, for the briefest of moments, telling her about the coating of supernatural oddness that had been plaguing her, but she snuffed the impulse. Everything around her was jumping and moving to the beat of everyday normalcy and her fear now seemed groundless. Besides, if the woman wasn't superstitious, she'd probably think she was crazy. "I'm fine. Just a little transition stress, I suppose."

"Did you find out if your uncle had any outstanding debts or problems?"

Rowan shrugged. "Not really. Doesn't seem important now."

The older woman studied her, as if trying to decide if she spoke the truth before glancing beyond her. "Looks like you have a fan club."

Turning, Rowan winced as Justin beamed toward her from his side of the bar. The light only dimmed when he had to mix up a drink for a customer. Behind him, Luke watched, expression a little too neutral. "He's … sweet…"

"But annoying?"

"I didn't say that."

"You didn't have to. How are things going with the surly bartender who lives in your storage room?"

"We're … co-existing."

Margie eyed her for a long moment, a smile flitting across her face. She nodded as if coming to some internal conclusion. "Lack of bloodshed is always a good sign."

Uncomfortable, Rowan peered around, noting craned necks her way. "Listen, Margie, I hate to cut this short, but I'm starting to get the stink eye from some of my customers, but maybe we could get together sometime soon for lunch. Right now, though, is there anything I can grab for you...?"

Margie swirled a cocktail at her. "I think I'm good for now. Go take care of your business."

Rowan continued her circuit, replenishing drinks, checking burger orders, and trying to dodge extra-friendly hands, unsuccessful at her last table when an inebriated customer cupped her ass. Abruptly turning and pulling away, she shot him a narrow-eyed look that had him dropping his own gaze in shame. He shifted from her annoyed eyes to stare at the wall and sulk.

Luke had one of her drink orders waiting, throwing up a brow when she leaned against the bar. "Seems you have your hands full out there."

"I can handle it."

"I noticed."

She gazed at him, a little surprised to see the glint of anger in his eyes, but to his credit, he said nothing. Very wise. The last thing she needed was her bartender going Neanderthal on a drunken customer with frisky fingers.

Luke jerked his head and she moved closer, barely suppressing a shudder when his warm breath tickled her ear. "I wanted to let you know that Dave got back to me."

Rowan stared at him for a moment before awareness echoed dully. The normalcy of the evening left on one heavy sigh. "Oh."

"Right now they're in Florida but will be heading back the day after tomorrow. She's agreed to meet with us, but suggests you stay close to home for the time being."

"I'm starting to feel stupid about this."

Luke reached out and rested his hand over hers for the shortest of moments, his flesh warm against hers. "Growing up in this area, you hear a lot of superstition, but Mrs. Leroux has always been amazing at splitting fact from fiction. Give her a chance." He shrugged. "Best-case scenario, she dispels some fear, worst case, she gives you some protection. Just don't take it lightly."

His gaze pressed against hers, his expression annoyingly neutral, eyes intense.

After a moment, she nodded. She already worried about her sanity, so there was little to lose.

"By the way, if that guy touches you again, he'll need a spotter to take a piss for a month." He smiled when she frowned at him.

Chapter Eighteen

The band had broken down their equipment, tossed down some complimentary beers, and now gradually moved everything out. A few regulars stuck around, but closing time ticked near, giving Rowan plenty of room to ponder her situation.

It had been better when they'd been busy. Zipping around kept the worry at arm's length, but now, thoughts crowded her brain, dark and unwanted. The steady thump of a headache rose from the base of her skull and she rubbed at it, distracted.

The day had been insane. Just that morning, she and Luke had ridden out in search of his shaman, or whatever the hell she was. Then there was Henry lying in a hospital bed while his family waited for a miracle. And then there was … Luke.

Squeezing her eyes closed, Rowan pressed harder at the ache in her head, wishing to dispel her uneasiness and turmoil. He was one more complication she hadn't counted on.

When she opened them, she glanced over to find his gaze affixed to her. A tingle ran down her spine and she looked away, trying to appear casual, doubting she did. After their earlier rainy day kiss, she didn't know if she could ever gaze at him again without that shudder of want coursing through her. She would never have allowed such a public display of affection before. Sudden awareness brought heat to the surface of her skin.

But as complicated as Luke seemed to be, she wanted to believe that he'd never be the kind of man to promise her a future while screwing her best friend on the side.

That day came back to her, and she shook her

head. She'd dropped by Craig's place with a bottle of wine, let herself in with the key he'd entrusted to her, and, well, things hadn't gone well. Primitive sounds led her to a sight that had Rowan taking her vino and leaving even as her fiancé had struggled into his pants to follow her.

The humiliation still burned her. She hadn't returned his ring, choosing to hock it instead. Childish, maybe, but she held no regret.

"How're you doing?" Luke swung onto the bench seat opposite her, glass of bourbon in hand. "Don't know if you noticed while sitting here with that dead-eyed stare, but we've been closed for a while now."

Rowan blinked and looked around. The dining room was deserted and she couldn't even detect Sonny's off-key singing from the kitchen either. Except for the steady hum of the AC, the place was silent.

"Everybody already left?"

"Yeah." He took a drink, eyes on her. "When you were zoning."

She gazed down into her soda and pushed it around with one finger. "There's too much trying to crowd itself into my brain at once. I don't think there's enough room in there."

He nodded, his mouth turning upward for a moment before leveling out. "You should probably get some rest. It's been an … eventful … day."

"Fat chance." Rowan made no move to get up, just continued to push the unfinished soda around the table. "I keep expecting to wake up, like I'm living a dream within a dream one minute. The next minute I think I'm being ridiculous, you know, making-mountains-out-of-molehills kind of thing."

Luke said nothing for a long moment, as if weighing whatever words were working their way through his head. He sighed. "Sometimes we get stuck in a nightmare. At least you can most likely escape yours."

She looked back up, gaze roaming his face. He stared at her blandly before focusing beyond her, throat working. Thinking about the tidbit of information her mother had passed to her, Rowan wasn't sure what to say, so waiting seemed the right response.

"I'm not sure how much Andy told you and I can only imagine what must be going through your head. When you called me a loser a while back—"

"I'm so sorry, Luke. I was upset, but I had absolutely no right to say that. It was cruel and uncalled for." Shame flooded over her at the memory and her belly tightened. Temper lashing out or not, it had been a shitty thing to say.

"You were right." He shrugged, bringing his gaze back to hers. "I wasn't always, but all it takes is that one … event … to shove you down a path you'd never have envisioned for yourself. Ever. 'Course, once you're heading that way, it's almost impossible to change direction."

"I don't believe that."

A smile twisted at the corner of his mouth. "That's easy enough to say."

"Maybe, but it's not like you're ninety. Things change and always will. It's inevitable."

"So all the platitudes assure us." He finished his drink, stared into the empty glass, and grimaced. "I used to have something to offer. I honestly did."

She waited, but he said nothing more. When silence stretched between them, she figured that was as close as he was going to get at the moment. Maybe, just maybe, he'd feel free to open up later and tell her about his wife and daughter, but for now the door had closed. "It's okay, Luke. We all tend to hide the hurt, don't we?"

He didn't look at her, continuing to stare into his glass. The muscles in his jaw flexed, betraying his tension.

Hoping to lighten the mood, Rowan cleared her throat and climbed to her feet. She slid him a glance from the corner of her eye and smirked. "In other news, I've decided to introduce a karaoke night to The Goose."

He went blank before his brows crinkled in consternation. When he looked up at her, the expression of absolute horror made her laugh. It felt good.

"Seriously?"

She shrugged, happy for the moment of brevity. "It's fun. Have you ever done it?"

****

He stared at her as she wandered over to the jukebox, perused for a few seconds, and selected a couple songs. "Don't you ever sing along when a favorite song comes on?"

She turned and offered him such a beautiful smile that his insides pooled. Realization cascaded over him and he pulled in a full, but shaking, breath.

"Not if I can help myself." It occurred to him what she was doing and he shook his head, touched, amused, and something more. He'd almost told her about Catherine and McKenzie, but the words stuck in his throat. They'd festered there, almost choking him. Instead of pushing him to unburden himself, she chose to distract. Just like he'd done to her earlier at the café.

Rowan began to sing along with Lucinda Williams, keeping in tune with the singer's throaty voice. Luke blinked in surprise, fairly impressed. If all karaoke singers sang that well, he would have less of a problem with it. When she grabbed a bottle of hot sauce off a neighboring table to use as a mic, he couldn't contain the slow smile taking over his face.

Hope spread throughout his body and he realized the trouble he was in as he watched the floor show. Her rich, cherry hair bounced against her slim shoulders when she moved to the music, mouth twitching with good humor as her gaze remained on him.

Johnny Cash came on next and she offered him the hot sauce. "C'mon, you need to take over. We both know I won't be able to do Johnny any justice."

Luke got up and walked over to take the bottle but chose to place it on a nearby table instead of crooning into it. Her playful smile fell ever so slightly when he touched her hair, resting his hand between her neck and the crook of her shoulder. He brushed her jaw with his thumb, marveling at the velvety softness of her skin.

From the moment she'd walked into the bar, he'd wanted her. Anger over the realization had been his first, natural response. Now there was no anger, only a bittersweet acceptance.

Those gray eyes pinned him now, watching, a little leery, smile gone.

He framed her face, hands caressing her cheeks, knowing he was a goner. He'd fallen harder than he would have ever believed possible. But there was no way to articulate it to her. He needed more time.

Words lost, he angled his head downward. The first kiss was tentative, asking, knowing where it might lead tonight. Knowing where he wanted it to lead. The emotions balled inside hadn't been so insistent since his wife. No other woman had evoked this kind of raw want and attraction. He kissed her again and felt her fade into him, one hand sliding up to his shoulder, the other pushing into his hair.

She pressed her body to his and he succumbed to burgeoning emotions instead of whatever may come tomorrow morning. Caressing his lips with hers, merging and falling deeper, he felt his needs burning brighter.

Appearing to come to a decision, she broke away and took his hand.

****

Luke's midnight-blue eyes had bled into onyx, but his face tensed, looking a little unsure. It wasn't an expression he comfortably wore. She suspected she knew why.

As always, he wore a long-sleeved shirt. Another Henley, unbuttoned below the throat, but no further. Hiding his scars must have become second nature.

"It's okay," she whispered, pressing her palm harder against his, twining their fingers. She didn't know exactly what the warmth in her belly was telling her, but she didn't believe it would lead her wrong. At least not tonight.

He followed her, and when they reached the base of the stairs, he pulled her off her feet and into his arms. Rowan cradled the back of his head, pressing her lips to his as he carried her. They stepped through the essence of roses, but neither broke the kiss.

Once inside the tiny apartment, he hesitated, resting his forehead against hers. "Are you sure about this?"

Her mind whirled, but she nodded. "As long as you have protection, we're good."

His mouth pulled to the side in a smirk. "I'm a guy. I always have protection."

Rowan huffed but pulled him in for another kiss before he allowed her to drop to her feet. Their eyes met as they stilled, regarding one another, nerves trembling to the surface.

Taking the rare initiative, she caught the hem of his shirt in both hands and peeled it upward. His body froze, but he did nothing to prevent her from removing the garment and tossing it aside. The planes of his chest were hard and lean, skin smooth on the undamaged side, pink and raised where he was scarred. A low moan rattled from him, deep and pained, but she ignored him, choosing to press her lips to his past injuries while he closed his eyes.

"You don't have to…"

"I want to. You are who you are." It was true. Everyone was a hot mess of scars and she was no exception. Most of hers just pressed from the inside out.

Luke allowed her gentle touches for a few moments before catching her by the upper arms and holding her gaze with his. He must have approved of what he saw because his mouth turned hot and hard against hers, taking her startled breath with it.

He picked her up and walked to the bedroom before they both tumbled into the softness of her comforter. From above her, Luke brushed her hair behind one ear, eyes dark with desire, but his gentle touch not more than a kiss upon her skin. A tenderness she hadn't felt in a very long time bloomed low and spread through her bloodstream. She traced the contours of his face with her fingertips, memorizing the softness of his skin, the tiny dimple when he smirked, the straightness of his nose, and brush of his stubble.

Retreating, he reached out to pull her into a sitting position to skim her top up over her head, his gaze roaming over the blue of her sports bra and the curve of her breasts.

Rowan stripped the garment off, meeting his eyes, amused as his jaw sagged. He recovered in bare moments, pressing forward to kiss her neck, hand lightly running over her, igniting her skin beneath. She sucked in a breath when he worked his way down her sternum to plant open-mouthed kisses across her breasts, before sucking one nipple into his mouth and flicking it with the tip of his tongue. He kissed the tautness of her belly, unzipped her jeans, and slid his fingers within. He chuckled when she jerked in surprise.

Luke hooked his fingers in her waistband to pull her bottoms and panties clear, and proceeded to caress her thighs with hands, lips, and tongue. When he slid up to her juncture, she dropped her head back against the pillows and sucked in a long, searing breath.

Dizziness and pleasure soared within her mind and body. She floated, still amazed how gentle this man was. He'd pulled off the ultimate con on her. Luke wasn't anything like he'd pretended.

Sweat and gooseflesh rose over her skin and she blinked and shuddered. When he nudged her over the first peak, she arched upward, her body tensing and flooding with release.

A true smile broke across his face when he crept up to brace above her. "God, you're beautiful, Rowan."

"I bet … you say that … to … every woman … you sleep with…" She returned his smile, breaths coming in quick puffs between words.

"Sure." Luke's smile quirked to the side before disappearing and his voice dropped to a whisper. "This time it happens to be true."

He pressed another kiss to her lips, burning and tingling against her. Luke nuzzled against her throat and she closed her eyes, letting the steady thrum of heat mingle with the lightness of bliss. Part of her wondered if it was just a snippet from a highly erotic dream. When he nipped her lower lip and offered her a roguish grin, the lovely haze split with a bolt of electricity. Her need burst from within and every negative thought entertained slipped away. Luke filled her senses, leaving everything else an unimportant blur.

Rowan helped him shuck his jeans and boxer briefs, their movements faster, more insistent. Mouths met, kisses frantic, tongues touching and then tangling. When he slid inside, she was more than ready, but she couldn't bite back her gasp as he filled her.

Luke stopped to give her time to acclimate, but she smiled, pulling him down to crush her lips to his. She nipped him back as she wrapped herself around him, his slow rocking exploding into sudden powerful thrusts. Rowan shifted her hips to meet him eagerly, bringing him further inside her. As her blood pressure soared and sweat slicked her skin, she marveled how well they fit together. Hanging on to his shoulders, her sight dimmed and flickered when her muscles tensed. Second later, the tight ball of energy deep within her loins crackled and radiated outward in an explosive burst of heat and pleasure. A soft cry escaped from between her lips, lights dancing behind her eyes. Some part of her was aware of a tiny noise emanating from Luke's throat when his own climax overtook him. He settled over her, breathing harsh, but despite his weight, she held him close, brushing her lips over his brow.

They lay together, saying nothing for several moments until he rolled away to dispose of the condom, returning to her side before cool air could rush in to replace him. He pulled her close, and she rested her cheek to his chest, listening to his heart beat, feeling his breath against her hair.

Muscles relaxing, her mind fuzzed with sleepiness. Through the fog, she wondered if she'd regret her actions, but she dozed off before her brain could formulate an honest answer.

Chapter Nineteen

"Well, kiddo. You're all grown up." Jimmy tilted his head, regarding her. Deep creases slashed into his face, while dark circles beneath gray eyes offered a cadaverous appearance. Brushes of gray-tinged ginger hair stuck out at odd angles as if electrocuted and still carrying voltage.

Rowan sat at the bar down from her uncle, gazing at him with trepidation. She'd never been afraid of him before, and the new realization baffled and saddened her. She had so many questions, but she couldn't seem to find her voice.

"You look just like your mom." He smiled, tone self-deprecating. "Good thing. She got the attractive genes. I wound up looking like your great-aunt Tilly. Believe me, she was a scary woman, that one."

When she continued to study him, he sighed. "I'm sorry, Rowan. I fucked up. Sorry about the swearing. I mean, I messed up. This is really hard. I can't even tell you. I'm still working stuff out, being dead and all. I tried to get your attention with the chair thing, but I guess all I did was succeed in scaring the hell out of you instead. I'm sorry about that, too."

She blinked at him. "That was you? I thought it was Robert."

Jimmy made a phhtt sound between his lips. "Nah, that guy is a one-hit wonder. Not that I can blame him. Once you get something down, you kind of stay with what works. The woman is kind of like that, too. Timothy tends to be a lot quieter, but he's still adjusting."

"Timothy."

"I guess he hasn't shown himself to you yet. He

might not for a few years, well, if he even sticks around."

"This is so weird," she mumbled, trying to remember what she was doing before she landed at the bar talking to her dead uncle. For whatever reason, her mind was blank.

"I'm going to have to make this fast, kiddo. Communicating this way takes a lot out of, well, both of us. It would be easier if you were a sensitive, but it doesn't feel like that's the case."

"Sensitive?" The word slurred, and she didn't know why. She tried again. "What do you mean by sensitive?"

He'd paled, shadows sinking deeper in, the bones of his face jutting. "I don't have much time. I need to show you something. Will you come with me?"

Rowan didn't move, frowning at him instead. Her brain seemed to be tilting and she shook her head to right it. "I don't know."

"It'll help you understand. I really am sorry. Sorry for so many things. You have no idea how much." Anguish sharpened his appearance into just short of terrifying and Rowan found herself sliding off the stool and backing away. "You might even hate me, but I have to take that chance. You need to know the truth."

"Please." Fear glazed the eyes so much like her own. "He might try to break through again soon. You should see before he does."

He appeared to be fading, and she blinked her eyes hard to clear them. "He? The man who's been … haunting me?"

"Come with me now." Jimmy reached out to take her hand.

****

Luke opened one eye at the first loud strike but waited a moment to judge whether it came from his subconscious or reality. Sleep had been sound for the first time in months, maybe even years, and he was reluctant to leave it behind. Reaching out to stroke one hand across Rowan's smooth skin, all he touched were cool sheets and tangled bedding.

He sat up quickly at the second blow, the pounding emulating from the other side of the wall. Pulling on his underwear, he stepped into the living room, cautious, but half-expecting it to be one of the tavern's ghosts yanking his chain.

Switching on the lamp next to the couch, he froze and stared in bewilderment.

Rowan swung the hammer into the drywall, the small hole she'd created gradually expanding into a gaping opening between studs. She hit the wall again, face slack, emotionless.

"Rowan?"

She didn't respond, the swinging of the hammer steady, the force used evenly distributed.

Sleepwalking? She'd been coherent enough to pull his shirt on but nothing else. In almost any other circumstance, he would have been amused and a trifle turned on at the sight of her perfect butt cheeks peeking out and flashing at him.

His heart kicked up and an icy chill settled onto his skin when understanding slapped at him. She was reopening one of the holes Jimmy had punched into the wall before his death.

Breath rasping in his ears, he stepped forward, gaze secure on Rowan. She seemed unaware of his presence, the blows from the hammer continuing, evenly spaced. Those beautiful smoky eyes stayed distant, unfocused. Her hair was tucked behind one ear, but tumbled down past her shoulders in sleep-tousled waves.

When he reached her, he gently took the hammer

from her hand and placed it on the coffee table. Her arms dropped to her sides, but she continued to face the wall.

"Rowan?" Was he even supposed to touch her? Was it a bad thing to touch a sleepwalker? He tried to remember but couldn't. "Why don't you go back to bed? It's too early to get up."

She hesitated before turning and looking straight through him. Luke shivered at the emptiness of her eyes, remembering how full of mischief and passion they'd been just a short couple of hours earlier. Stepping past him, she returned to the bedroom.

Luke followed in time to see her slip under the covers and curl on her side. Her soft breathing reached his ears a moment later, slow and steady.

Perplexed but curious, he returned to the impressive hole she'd made. Dust and plaster littered the floor between the couch and the French doors, some powdered fragments still hanging in the air. On a hunch, he tried to peek inside but was only met with darkness.

He knew Rowan had that big-ass flashlight in here somewhere and spent a few moments looking for a logical spot. Not under the sink in the kitchen. Not in the tiny pantry next to the fridge. Not braced in a corner somewhere. Where the hell would she put it? He had no clue.

Returning to the hole, he took a chance and reached inside, hoping to hell he wouldn't get bitten by a brown recluse spider or something. His fingertips brushed the corner of what felt like a book and he stretched a few millimeters more while the edge of the drywall pressed into his armpit. He caught it between his thumb and forefinger and managed to pull it up without dropping it.

It was just a simple journal. The red cover was torn and battered but otherwise it seemed intact. For better or worse, somehow Rowan had been guided to it. Luke studied the book clenched in his hand, debating whether he should overstep and read it. Decided the next second he sure as hell would. It might piss her off, but he was willing to deal with her reaction.

Fear for her became a twisting cold spot at the base of his spine and the need to protect her overshadowed everything.

He stepped back into the bedroom to check on her, relieved to find her still sleeping deeply. Leaning down, he touched his lips to the top of her head before returning to the living room.

Chapter Twenty

Early-morning sun sifted through the blinds to warm her face. The blur of orange glowed from beyond her closed lids and she turned over, seeking muted darkness and a little bit more sleep. Somewhere in her sluggish brain, she contemplated the use of blackout shades. It would make sense. She did run a bar after all. With a soft sigh, Rowan reached out, craving contact. She cracked open her eyes when she didn't find it.

The sheets and blanket were cool.

Disappointment and more hurt than she wanted to think about sunk into her chest. Just like that, he'd gone. Bastard obviously got what he wanted.

She sat up, suddenly aware of the maroon Henley draped over her. His shirt. Way too large, it slid off her shoulder. She had no memory of pulling it on. The last thing she recollected was drifting off curled against him, the aroma of soap, sweat, and lovemaking heady in her nose.

The prospect of more sleep gone, she climbed from bed, pausing to pull on a pair of shorts, and padded out into the living room. Blinking to clear her eyes, she had coffee in mind, but thoughts of Luke pushed to eclipse it. Pain of his desertion reverberated inside and she pressed her lips together, irritated that they'd begun to tremble. It surprised her to find her eyes stinging, and she blinked back the emotions with the tears.

Rowan gasped and stumbled back when she found the man sitting on her couch in his boxer briefs, staring beyond the dark television. Exhaustion and tension pulled at his face, eyes faraway. His jaw throbbed when he tilted his head up toward her.

"You startled me. I thought you left." She rested a

hand to her chest in emphasis, feeling a little guilty and a little stupid. What did they say about making assumptions? Maybe it was time to work on giving certain folks the benefit of the doubt. "Why are—" She cut herself off as she stared past him. "What the hell did you do to my wall?"

The drywall caved into a dark hole a good eight or ten inches in circumference. Plaster, paint fragments, and dust formed an untidy pile at the baseboard.

Luke squinted at her, expression blank.

Bewildered, she glanced from him to the damage and back again. "What?"

"Any dreams last night?"

"What are you talking about?" She stepped toward the back wall, reaching out to touch the edge of the ragged hole. "Decide to redecorate or something?"

"No."

Rowan shifted, gaze landing on him, falling a moment later to the coffee table. A hammer rested across a couple of dog-eared magazines, its head coated in white dust. A deep frigidity rose up from her blood, a wave of dizziness right behind. She searched her memory from the night before, but any dreams she may have had stayed out of reach, barely shadows skirting her subconscious. "I did that?"

He watched her, rising when a second wave of dizziness made her reach out to steady herself against the wall. Luke curled an arm around her shoulders, bringing her down to the sofa, sitting beside her. "You were sleepwalking."

She frowned and stared down into her lap where her hands twisted around one another in war. Pulling them apart, she slid them under her thighs to still the incessant movement as she searched her memory. "I've never done that before."

"You were being directed. I think someone or something wanted you to find this." He reached across to the coffee table to pick up a small red journal.

She stared at it without recognition before her gaze rose to find his. The chill stayed inside, fear and confusion swirling through it. "I presume you read it."

Luke nodded. "I'm not going to apologize."

"I wouldn't expect you to." She took it from his hand, meeting his gaze. "Do I even want to know?"

"You might consider fastening your seatbelt and leaving your structured reality at the door."

"That good, huh?"

"Riveting." The worry hadn't left his face, but a new softness touched his eyes. He ran a hand over her hair, twisting a thick strand around his finger. "Honestly, I wish you wouldn't read it, but I know you need to."

She smiled at him, but the frost inside had yet to dissipate. She expected it to get worse. Flipping through, she noted there were very few entries. The first was dated six months before his death.

February 6

There's nowhere for me to turn. No one could possibly understand and I can't bear the thought of my few friends looking at me as a monster. After all, I made my bed and all that. Writing this down won't accomplish anything, other than maybe ease an old man's conscience a little, so here it goes.

When I met Marcus Ady, it was an innocent enough association. Of course, I didn't know what he was or what he was capable of. I didn't know he was the devil. Honestly, how could I? We met in the underground. The tourist shops are all bullshit and I was looking for something stronger. This bone thing was getting worse and some days I could barely move. I tried to hide it, but I can't say how hard it's been. The doctors are full of crap with their constant waffling. Maybe this. Maybe that. The only drugs I'm not allergic to hadn't done squat so I decided to try something else.

He offered to help me with his own form of treatment for free, at least at first. I suppose it was a try before you buy. At least that's what I was thinking at the time. We began to meet in different locations with his little bag of tricks. He gave me something to take. It was some kind of powder under my tongue. He'd draw these symbols in the dirt, light candles, speak in some kind of foreign language. I'm not sure what it was, but it wasn't anything I'd ever heard before. My head became muddled at first, but it wore off and I felt so light, almost like I was floating. My brain was so open, everything seemed clearer somehow. I swear I could practically hear bugs screwing. I felt young, invincible. And the best part is that the pain was gone. Completely gone.

I go back to him now. I can't help myself. It's such a high. I've never felt so good in my life. My body and mind crave it like an addiction. In the beginning, I didn't even think about payment. But he knew what he was doing. Oh yes. He's gotten me hooked, so when he asked tonight, it made me sick, but I couldn't say no.

Turns out, the devil isn't exactly immortal. At least not without help. And that's what he wants from me.

May 13

I can't keep doing this but the devil won't let me go. I'm so damned scared. It's not worth it anymore. All those innocents. Some little more than children. Street people. Mentally ill people. He tells me they're suffering. Maybe they are, but it's not for him to decide their fate. When I watch these people let go, I feel sick. I would have expected screams, but they're quiet, almost peaceful. But it doesn't matter. Their blood is on me just the same. He's becoming stronger. I can feel it. He won't need me soon.

Sickness curled in her stomach, but Rowan forced herself to continue to read to the last.

June 17
Tonight it ends. He can't get any stronger. Everyone should have a natural life span. Even him. He might kill me, and that's okay. I've accepted it. As long as I can release all those people, let them find their final rest, it'll be worth it. I've been watching, waiting. I think I know how to do it. It has to be the talismans. He believes my obedience, my need. He won't expect it from me.

August 2
Even weakened, he's after me. He's so angry. Luckily, he avoids The Goose. I can't understand it, but the spirits here try to protect me, or maybe it's even something about the building. I don't know for sure, but I do know there are some cracks in the defense. I stay inside, but he can still get in my head. Sometimes in dreams, sometimes when I'm awake. He makes me see things. Horrible things. I know he wants my energy. The link is too strong. The blood and soul of an enemy is a powerful elixir. It would heal him, and I can't let that happen, for my sake, for anyone else's. When I die, I need to take him with me. My friends and customers are starting to look at me funny now. Luke is concerned, but I can't tell him what I've done. That's the last thing the boy needs. I don't know how long I can hold on…
****

Luke watched the color drain from her face entry by entry. He wanted nothing more but to throw her on the back on his Harley and leave the city, leave the state and head for destinations unknown. But he instinctively knew that wouldn't happen. Running couldn't resolve this.

"Marcus Ady. I haven't heard the name before."

"Neither have I, but I'm going to look into it."

A weak smile tried to yank at her full lips, her perfect cupid's bow twitching. "I guess the rest of this might make sense to you? Is forewarned, forearmed?"

But it didn't make sense to him. He'd believed the man haunting her was a bokor, but what Jimmy described seemed to be something more. Something worse. "It'll make sense to Mrs. Leroux." At least he hoped to hell it did.

"How can you be so sure, Luke?" Her gaze fell from his before slowly returning, the question sounding tired.

He hedged. "She's an amazing lady. She knows her way around voodoo, sure, but she's also a sensitive. And Dave's a cop. Between all of us, we can figure this out."

Her brows drew into a frown of concentration, as if she were trying to remember something. "Sensitive."

"From the time she was a child. According to David, at least." He removed the journal from her and placed it back on the coffee table. "They'll be back tomorrow and we'll do whatever needs to be done."

"What if nothing can be done?" She stared at him listlessly.

He hated this. He hated what was happening. Allowing feigned annoyance to camouflage his fear and feelings for the woman, he scoffed at her. "What do you plan on doing? Are you going to wait around until the worst happens? Seriously, Rowan, what the fuck?"

Startled, she stared at him until the stark white of her face colored in temper and she clenched her fists. Her eyes darkened into the color of thunderheads. "Well, excuse me for not knowing how to react when someone or something wants me dead. If it even wants me dead. Sounds like it might be even worse. Whatever that might be. I came to this damn city for a fresh start after getting screwed over and here I am living in a haunted bar and being hunted by something … otherworldly. Maybe this is status quo or a typical Tuesday for you, but it's not exactly the norm for me."

Luke got to his feet and paced. "No, actually this is a typical Thursday for me. If it were Tuesday, the Rougarou would be stopping by for a beer, a bowl of Spanish peanuts, and a side order of redhead."

She'd stood up to follow in anger, but stopped, brow furrowing as her mouth dipped open. "What the hell is a Rougarou?"

Bewilderment clouded her face, and he couldn't hold the smile back. He stepped close and ran his hands up and down her arms. "Gotcha."

Sighing, she shook her head and leaned into him. "You're right. Wallowing does nothing."

He wrapped his arms around her, one hand skimming beneath the over-sized shirt to stroke the smooth skin of her back. "No, wallowing does nothing. However, I can think of a couple other things that are much more … enjoyable."

She looked up at him, fear still in her eyes but not quite as stark. A budding smile pressed into her mouth. "Really."

"Um hmm." Luke nuzzled her throat, enjoying the scent of her, the feel of goosebumps rising against her flesh. He wanted them both to shove the black cloud back into a pinpoint. At least for now. When he kissed her, she melted into it for a moment, but paused for the barest of seconds.

"Seriously, Luke. What is a Rougarou?"

"Cajun werewolf darlin'." He swallowed her tiny laugh with the next kiss.

Chapter Twenty-One

When Luke opened the door, he took a quick tumble back to the age of twelve. He recalled feeling similar at his grandmother's funeral. The presence of certain people seemed to hold that kind of power.

Ruth Leroux hadn't changed and he didn't know whether to be impressed or a little frightened. He kept the conflict behind his mask as he stepped forward to kiss her on the cheek. "Bon jour, stranger."

"Hello, Lukas." Her eyes probed his, face sobering from pleasure.

Did she know? Or was she able to sense loss? Unnerved, he couldn't say.

"It's been a long time."

"Grand-mere's funeral."

The woman nodded, sober. "Yes. Wonderful woman. You must miss her. She would have helped you deal with your loss."

Luke frowned, staring at her. Something deep in his heart tore a little and his breath went raspy. "You know. How?"

"You disappeared afterward." Not answering, her gaze sought his, calm, understanding.

A prickling of sweat itched at his hairline and he swiped it with the heel of his hand. "Not intentionally."

She nodded, squeezed his arm. "But now you're back and ready for a fight, yes?"

"I guess I am. Look." Luke lowered his voice. "Rowan doesn't know about Cate and McKenzie. I'm not ready for her to know."

Ruth smiled, sadness weaving through it. "She won't learn anything for me. Speaking of your lady, we need to put this situation on the table and see what could be done."

He wasn't surprised at her insinuation that there was more between Rowan and him than just an employer-employee relationship. As a young boy, he'd thought she was a benign witch. He still wasn't sure. Especially the benign part.

David Leroux held out a hand, clasping Luke's firmly but with pleasure. He was a tall, slender man with close-clipped black hair and an angular face. He smiled, but it didn't reach eyes clouded with sorrow. "How have you been doing, Luke?"

He had no intention of going there. He couldn't. "Concerned for my boss. She's pretty shaken. This … situation … is beyond anything I've ever even heard of before."

Taking the hint, Dave nodded. "Well, you know as well as I do that Mama's the person to talk to. Actually that's why we were in Florida. Someone needed this kind of help in Tampa."

"What, she freelances?" Luke allowed a tiny smile.

"Not exactly. Sometimes certain situations beckon her." He shrugged. "Most of the time she stays close to home. As independent as she is, she's nervous about traveling and I can't always take time off."

"You still a cop?"

"Until I'm dead. Or until I at least earn my pension." He stepped into the cool interior. "I ran that name you gave me."

"And?"

"And nothing. No criminal record, credit record, social security number, or anything for a man named Marcus Ady."

"Fuck."

"Yeah. But I'm not giving up."

Luke nodded, pulling the heavy door closed and pausing to lock it. "I really appreciate this. Well, let me get you a beer while you're still off duty."

"I wouldn't say no."

Luke crossed to the bar, shooting careful glances at Rowan as he pulled two drafts. As far as he could tell, there'd been no nightmares the previous night. He'd stayed awake far too long watching the woman sleep, cradled within his arms, emotions taut as wire. Crossing the line into lovers hadn't been something he'd anticipated, but now he was in over his head. The thought of losing her left him raw, shaky, an ulcer on his soul. He couldn't let it happen. Not a second time.

He caught her gaze and she offered him a reassuring smile before her attention was captured and held by the lady before her.

****

Rowan had to admit she was surprised. She'd expected someone tiny, wizened, even frail, not a person with such a commanding presence. Ruth Leroux was a tall, stately woman who moved with the fluidity of someone twenty years younger. Her hair was thick, white, and pulled back into a simple roll from a virtually unlined face. Any eccentricity only showed itself in the bright colorful flow of her blouse and skirt. Her eyes, the hue of bittersweet chocolate, swept the tavern with amusement and interest before landing on Rowan. "You have some protection already. You also have some relatively friendly spirits here."

David Leroux stood near, hands shoved in his pockets, eyes sharp and observant beyond the friendliness. According to Luke, the man had joined the force fourteen or fifteen years ago, and that knowledge made Rowan feel a little better. Maybe because it was something concrete, real, instead of wisps of superstition.

Of course, she was probably deluding herself. There was nothing concrete or real about any of this.

Ruth approached, reaching out to take Rowan's hands in hers. "Luke's told us a little of your recent trouble."

"I appreciate your thoughts about this, because honestly, I'm feeling a little bit out of my element." To say the least. Only obstinance and, now Luke, had kept her from screaming back home.

"And what element would that be?"

"Reality."

The woman chuckled, sincere pleasure flashing in her eyes. "I understand and I'm going to want you to tell me everything you know, remember, or suspect, but first—" She glanced over at Luke and raised her brows. "I see you boys are helping yourself to some early refreshment. How about some spirits for an old woman and a beautiful young lady?"

"Sazerac?"

She smiled, straight white teeth flashing. "Now, how would you remember that? You were just a little boy."

"You're impossible to forget, Mrs. Leroux."

"Good to know." She looked back at Rowan, her eyes shimmering, but deep within their silky darkness, Rowan caught the old wise soul gazing out. It was like a thousand comforting childhood memories and Rowan felt something inside her settle.

"Now let's have a seat, honey."

"I'm sorry. Of course." She led the older woman to her preferred corner booth and slid in, back to the wall.

Ruth Leroux sat opposite, folded her long hands together and studied her.

Trying not to fidget, Rowan returned the frank assessment, noting, with some surprise, one cartilage piercing, four ear piercings in her left ear and three in her right. Ruby, emerald, and diamond gemstones glimmered as the woman tilted her head.

"I contemplated an eyebrow piercing too, but my son"—she shot a narrow-eyed look toward the bar—"complained. I still might get one though." The older woman shrugged. "Just another eccentric old lady."

"You don't really strike me as old."

She threw her head back, her laughter rich and inviting. "You flatter me. I think you might even be sincere. I gather I'm not what you expected."

"No." Rowan admitted, lifting one shoulder and letting it drop. "I suppose not."

Luke brought over a couple of drinks, including a hurricane for Rowan. She looked up, met his eyes, and watched his smile form from beyond his usual impassive expression. Conscious of their fledgling relationship, the flutter of an electric tingle sparked low in her belly. She nodded her thanks.

"Ah, the boy is a beverage artist." Ruth shifted her gaze between the two of them before she took a sip. Nodding with a hum of approval, she waved him away with a careless flick of her fingers. "Hollywood would cast me as … hmmm … short, wide, have an elfish voice and too much lipstick, maybe. What do you think?" The woman smiled with a touch of irony. "They might actually get the clothes right, though. Life's too short for boring."

A tiny bit embarrassed, Rowan said nothing. That was exactly what she'd envisioned.

"Okay, honey, let's see what I can pick up from you and then I'd like a tour of this lovely old building. We'll go from there, okay?" Smiling, Ruth reached out and took her hands, cradling them in those long, elegant ones that flashed rings on six of her digits. They were at once soft and strong, and Rowan felt confidence in the older woman's grip. Comfort warmed her as Ruth met and held her gaze for several minutes without words.

Finally, she pursed her lips, concern edged with a little fear crossing the woman's face. "The man has already left a few marks on you."

Rowan's mind wandered, feeling her face warm, and the older woman allowed a tiny smile in empathy. "Not Lukas, although he has, too. This other one. He's made of dark magic. He leaves the marks to weaken you, your judgment, your confidence. We'll keep him from leaving any more, but you need to trust me. Can you do that?"

She stared into the older woman's clear, direct eyes, that sense of comfort returning. A little numb, she nodded.

****

Luke sat at the bar with David, watching the man's body language as he paged through the journal.

"It was in the wall?"

"Yeah, that last night when Jimmy seemed to go nuts. He left a couple of holes. Fist-size holes. Didn't occur to me to look inside before I patched them up."

"And Rowan found it?"

"Someone here guided her. Maybe it was even her uncle. In fact, considering everything, that's damned likely. She was sleepwalking and couldn't remember any of her dreams."

Dave pursed his lips and pulled his brows together in thought. "Huh. Why the hell would he hide it in the wall?"

Luke took a long pull of his beer. "I've had a couple thoughts on that. Number one, he could have been afraid someone would come across it. What he wrote isn't all that specific, but it is damning no matter how you look at it. Or maybe he was hallucinating that the bokor was coming for him and panicked."

Despite the cool eyes of the cop, an underlying tension had his jaw throbbing. David read through a second time before pressing his lips together. "I'm not sure what to think about this. I haven't heard of a bokor with this much power. Could it have been in Jimmy's head, at least to some degree? You'd said his behavior changed."

Shoving one hand through his hair, Luke glanced over at the two women, focusing on Rowan before returning his attention to Dave. "Maybe a chicken or egg thing? Was he crazy before or did this bokor drive him crazy? Hard to say, isn't it? I can only say that the man went through some changes. Personality wise, Jimmy was an optimist, annoyingly so. At least since I knew him. Nothing bothered him, but he changed those last six or seven months." Luke smiled without mirth. "He started to behave more like me. Depressive, moody. Then he was up again—I figure that was the high part of his journal. Then the fear and erratic behavior, which matches the rest. Whether it was something already inside him, some kind of mental illness coming to the surface, I don't know. Maybe the bokor served as a catalyst and Jimmy just snapped. But..." He leaned forward, tension locking his muscles. "I don't think it's in Rowan's head too."

Dave gave him a long look before taking a sip of his beer. He wiped away imagined foam from his lips with the back of his hand. "I'm not much for coincidences."

"Neither am I." Luke found his gaze drifting back to Rowan before snapping back.

"You really care for that girl."

"I guess I do." He shrugged, ignoring the unasked

question. "No one deserves this."

"Look, I'm going to make some inquiries, tug some lines and see if I can come up with something more." He lowered his voice. "This guy, whoever he is, has to get his supplies somewhere. He may have given someone, somewhere, a bad vibe."

"Unless he makes all his own stuff."

Dave sighed. "Possible, but unlikely. At least not everything. Ingredients for some of the more heavy-duty spells are pretty rare. I think if someone came into one of the underground shops looking for certain things, he'd set off a buzz. Maybe even a panic, depending on what it was."

"If this guy was noticed, you think you can get folks to actually open up and share?" Luke knew damned well how superstitious and fearful people could get in the area. The idea of incurring a bokor's wrath was not something they'd knowingly do.

"I think so. I might be a cop, but I'm also one of them." He smiled, almost sheepishly. "Even if I couldn't, Mama sure could. She can make anyone talk … possibly even sing and do the chicken dance."

Luke allowed a ghost of a smile. "Yeah, I can see that." He sobered quickly, lowering his voice. "I have to admit this scares the shit out of me. There are too many parallels to Jimmy … and I can't stand the thought…"

He finished his beer with David watching him.

"There are never any guarantees, Luke. You know that. Sometimes people slide away despite everything."

"And that's what terrifies me."

"Do you love her?"

Not answering, he shifted to gaze at the two women. Snatches of conversation drifted his way. Little details that Rowan hadn't shared with him. "I don't know."

Straightening, Dave pulled out his cell. "Let me continue rolling the ball on my end. Talk with some folks I know. See if I can't flush someone or something out."

Chapter Twenty-Two

Ruth wandered through the tavern, stopping here and there, her eyes going in and out of focus. The old woman kept her hands out, fingers splayed, as if detecting heat from a stove. Her movements at times seemed erratic, other times, methodical. She'd stride from one area to another, long legs eating up distance quickly and efficiently, only to slow to a crawl, rotate, contemplate, and stare at nothing. Occasional words drifted from between her lips, entwining English and French. Sometimes she spoke dreamily in a language unrecognizable. On the second inspection of the building, she became much more aware and intent on her actions, not unlike a general with a plan of attack. She laid thick lines of coarse salt across every outside entrance, including windows, before going from top to bottom a third time. The third round involved candles, incense, some kind of herbal mixture, and small drawings of unfamiliar symbols on walls connecting to the outside.

Fascinated, Rowan followed at a distance. She'd been instructed by not only Ruth, but Luke and David, to not interfere as the woman toured and treated the old building, but she couldn't help but observe. She'd told her everything and the woman had listened with an open ear and a genuineness in her eyes that Rowan wasn't accustomed to. She hadn't looked at her like she was crazy.

Her parents would have just taken her to a psychiatrist. Hell, they would have had her committed.

"Ah, you're hiding. Shy are you?" Returning downstairs from the apartment once more, Ruth paused and spoke into the thin air of the kitchen. She tilted her head, the beginning of a smile playing around her lips before falling away. Ruth's face sobered into compassion. "I'm sorry, honey. I can feel your sadness. Just know that no one here's going to hurt you. And we appreciate your patience until this is over."

Rowan peeked into the small room, trying to see or feel something, anything, but there was nothing. Mavis was the only spirit that made its presence known to her on a semi-regular basis. Or was it Josephine, the woman who sacrificed herself for her daughter? She couldn't help but wonder.

Ruth sat down with her and held her hands once more, eyes forthright, instead of dreamy and elsewhere. They now burned with intensity and Rowan shivered. "With all these marks, these mind games, the bokor has been trying to exhaust you, push you to drop your defenses. That's what they do. When you're at your most vulnerable, he'd try to take you. What I've done here is fill in the cracks. He won't be able to get to you any longer, at least not while you're within these walls."

Rowan gaped at her. "I can't spend the rest of my life hiding in here. Being a prisoner is not living."

"Honey, I would never suggest you do that, but for the time being, I have something I want you to wear or keep on your person whenever you go outside. It'll help keep him from getting inside your head." She reached into her satchel, pulled out a small tied cloth pouch, and pressed it into Rowan's hand.

"For how long?"

The woman sighed. "My feeling is he's weak and may not have much time left. That's why he's so desperate." Her gaze flickered past Rowan and landed on Luke leaning against the bar. "It also makes him much more dangerous, so we can't underestimate him either."

"No, we can't." Dave stood near, his arms folded across his chest. "I was telling Luke that I think I'm also going to do some poking around, see if I can't get some kind of line on this bastard myself. His name may not be on record, but it could be in someone's head. This kind of presence wouldn't have gone unnoticed."

Ruth stared hard at him before slowly nodding and returning her attention to Rowan. "We both have our methods and can work toward the middle. Our prime objective is to keep you safe. Keep the gris-gris on you. It'll help protect you."

Rowan nodded, blankly staring down at the little cloth sack nestled in her palm. They all seemed so sure, but her cynical side still questioned. She tried her best to squash the doubt.

The old woman gave Luke a wave and he approached, dropping to his haunches by the table. She pushed another tiny bag toward him. "You too. He could use you to get to her. You need to be vigilant."

Nodding, he took it and slipped it into the front pocket of his trousers.

"Also, while the protection spells I've cast won't allow anything in, they also won't allow anything out, so your four spirits are trapped here for the time being. One was a little uncomfortable with it, but he, they, do understand."

Blinking, Rowan glanced at Luke, who frowned in bemusement, before returning her attention to Ruth. "Four?"

Ruth nodded. "Three males, one female. Two of them are old, well enmeshed in this building's history. I believe the female is the one who imparted the original protection spell, although I couldn't say what the how and the why might have been…"

"Josephine."

The older woman raised a brow. "Yes, that's the name I felt."

Rowan gave them a cursory overview of what she'd read regarding the history of the house and Luke folded his arms across his chest. "So much for Mavis."

Dismissing his comment, Ruth concentrated on Rowan. "The other two are new, very agitated, still getting their bearings, so to speak."

Images flickered behind Rowan's eyes, washed and faded, nothing distinct. Memories of a dream. Her uncle trying to tell her something. What the hell was it? She couldn't remember. "Jimmy's here, isn't he?"

"Yes, your uncle is here. The quiet one is also new."

"Okay, Jimmy is one of the new ones. That would make sense. He passed here. What about the other one?" Rowan shifted to Luke. "There wasn't another death here, I mean, in recent years, was there?"

"No, nothing."

"Sometimes spirits attach themselves to objects." Ruth pushed aside her empty glass. "That seems likely. It could be anything."

Rowan pondered for a long moment, her brain nudging up against overload. "Can you communicate with them?"

The woman smiled. "Not like I'm communicating with you. With spirits, it's more…" Her eyes drifted inward in reflection for a moment. "…like impressions and moods, although sometimes, if my mind is clear, I can get a little more from them."

"It gets cold when they get upset."

Ruth frowned, tilting her head. "One of them was angry with you?"

"No, I don't think it was me. I mean…" Rowan thought back to the moment, fighting the creeping heat up her neck at the memory of Luke's kiss. "Well, I was a little upset, confused. But I mentioned the man in my dreams and that seemed to set Mav—Josephine off. It got windy and the temperature dropped enough that I could see my breath. The next instant, it was gone."

"Hmmm … did you get the impression that it was fear? Or was it anger?"

"I'm not sure. My first thought was fear, but, well, I'm not exactly psychic or anything."

"Interesting." Ruth leaned back and the bench seat groaned. Her face pinched together in thought. "I've heard of some practitioners capturing spirits. They use wangas, which are basically talismans to store them for their own ends."

"Do you think that's what this man might be doing?" Rowan couldn't quite catch her breath, took a moment to pull one in slowly to steady herself. "What would someone do with a trapped spirit?"

"Power … renewal … I sense age and weakness in the marks he's left on you…" She continued, as if to herself. "There were tribes known to eat the flesh of the enemy to gain their strength…"

Cold, so cold. Ice crystals seemed to form in her blood, slowing it, freezing her from within. When Luke sat next to her, she wanted to lean against him but couldn't move. Her muscles tensed and ached. She couldn't really be hearing this, could she?

"Blood or soul of the enemy would be a potent elixir for him."

Where had she heard that?

Memories sifted in fits and starts. She'd had a dream, that was what is was. Jimmy had been talking to her. What had he said? It wouldn't come, other than his apologies. Those had been clear.

"So, because Jimmy betrayed this guy, somehow wounded him in the process, he needs a relative to balance the scales?" Luke looped an arm around

Rowan's shoulders, rubbing one hand up and down her bicep. His touch brought comfort and she broke her freeze and moved into his warmth, hating this feeling of weakness and trying hard to kindle the fire of her temper.

"Balance the scales? Maybe, but I think it might be more about survival." Ruth folded her hands, gazing across at both of them before zeroing in on her son. "David, I think it's necessary for you to go back a little further with this one."

"A little further?"

"I told you, I sense age." She narrowed her eyes. "Unnatural age."

Dave nodded, eyes already sharpening in thought.

Despite her own belly flipping around, Rowan didn't detect any surprise in the man's expression. She supposed not much knocked him off his equilibrium. She wished she could say the same for herself.

Ruth brought her attention back. "I want you to try not to worry. You're safe here and the gris-gris will help protect you out there."

A thought slid within the numbness in her brain and Rowan shifted her focus from Ruth back to David. "What if we let him come for me? Couldn't you arrest him then?"

His eyes softened in compassion, his voice low. "For what?"

Understanding was heavy and Rowan felt like she was falling. There was no evidence of anything, just the play of smoke and mirrors in her head and the rambling of her uncle in an old journal. Although he'd appeared to her several times, she couldn't even remember what the man looked like most of the time. Except his eyes. Those remained clear. Her mouth dry, heart hammering, she leaned forward. "If you let him take me, isn't that kidnapping?"

"Hell, no." Luke glared at her. "That is not going to happen."

She scowled, pulling away from him. "It's not your call."

"The hell it's not. I'll knock you out and tie you up myself if you even think about pulling something that stupid."

Bristling, temper bursting from a well of fear, Rowan bared her teeth. "Try it and see what happens, you jerk."

"Knock it off, both of you." David met her eyes and shook his head. "I'm sorry. I can't allow that. It's way too dangerous. Too many variables."

Rowan appealed to Ruth for any semblance of support, but the older woman shook her head as well. "Honey, I know you want this over with. I truly do understand, but serving yourself up as some kind of trussed-up turkey isn't the answer. Do what I ask for now, please, and my boy over there will tip over some rocks and see what squirms out. I even have some folks I can talk to. If we figure out who he really is and where he is, it takes away a lot of his advantage. You need to have patience."

Patient was the last thing she felt. Terrified stood at the top of the list in neon colors, but white-hot rage bumped up against it as a close second. She fisted her hands, body trembling.

Her emotions had to have been painted all over her face with clear, broad strokes because Ruth spoke to her with such gentleness. "I know you're scared and I wouldn't demean either of us by suggesting you shouldn't be, but please be willing to take a leap of faith and believe that we will do everything we can to end this nightmare for you. Trust that you have a lot working on your side."

She gazed across the table, soaking in the eccentricity fused with understanding and sincerity. Despite their heated words, Luke rested one hand on her leg and squeezed in reassurance as David nodded.

A second later a cool breeze brought the robust scent of roses.

****

Luke watched her as she continued to drown in that temper of hers. She spoke with customers, smiled and pretended, all while that knot in her jaw kept throbbing.

And she wouldn't look at him.

But that was okay. It wasn't the first time he'd endured the silent treatment and sure as hell wouldn't be the last. Without any kind of backup, she at least wouldn't attempt the stupid action she'd proposed.

The thought of it sent threads of panic through his belly and up his spine. He sucked in a full breath, then another to steady himself. He knew what he was getting into when'd he'd chosen not to hop on his bike and leave town. Now he was stuck.

Rowan crouched down next to one table, chatting with the elderly couple seated there. There was nothing forced about this particular interaction, her smile free and genuine. She nodded, reached out, and touched the woman's hand, patting the man's shoulder when she straightened. Returning to the bar, she ignored Luke and hailed Justin to request a bottle of wine befitting a fortieth anniversary. She analyzed the three he brought her, decided on the Sonoma Coast Chardonnay, and returned to the table with two glasses. The couple beamed up at her.

Luke stared, completely gobsmacked. There was no other word to describe it. The grace of her movements, the warmth of her smile, the way the lighting bounced against her hair, sparking like embers. All her inside beauty only served to augment her already perfect features.

Over the last few years he'd made an internal promise that he'd never leave himself vulnerable to another woman again, and yet here he was. Stupid but the damage was done. There was no going back. Some tiny part of him expected Cate might even approve.

When Zoe hailed her for change, Rowan slid from the dining room toward the office.

Seeing an opportunity, Luke left Justin at the helm and followed her, his desire to rectify the situation swelling within him. It brought on a slice of shame, annoyance, and a definite dent to his pride, but his need for her trumped his irritation.

She'd sealed herself in the office, no doubt locking it as she accessed extra cash. Without pause, he used his own key to let himself in, closing the door and leaning against it.

Rowan barely passed him a glance as she removed ones and fives from the small floor safe. "I don't have time for this, Luke. I have to get back out there."

"How long is this tantrum going to last?"

"Tantrums are for children. I happen to be busy right now." She closed the safe and rose to face him, eyes still like flint.

"Uh huh." He tilted his head, watching the flint spark, fascinated.

When she lifted her chin in defiance, Luke stepped closer. There was little room for her to retreat and she didn't even try. Her glare would have been withering for most men.

But Luke wasn't most men. Saying nothing, he reached out to take her free hand and waited for the blaze to burn out. He rubbed one thumb gently over her knuckles in a subtle attempt to hasten it.

When she continued to stare, he touched her face, lightly running his fingers down her cheek and across her jawline. "That was very sweet what you did for that old couple."

She blinked and her brow furrowed.

"I don't want to lose you, Rowan." He lowered his voice to a whisper.

"That's playing dirty," she muttered, a faint scowl crossing her face.

Luke stepped close, dipping his head to press his lips to her forehead. When she sighed and her body relaxed, he drew her against him.

She pressed her cheek to his chest. "I hate feeling helpless, Luke."

"I know." Helplessness was no stranger to him and he hated it just as much, if not more.

"You're an easy scapegoat now. You understand that, right?"

"Yeah."

When she met his gaze again, the flint and fire were gone. Fatigue stole in instead. "I want to sleep in peace. I want to be able to walk down the damned street, watching for muggers like a normal person. I don't want to fear that place behind my eyes where that guy seems to hover."

"I know." He pushed a hand through her hair, tangling his fingers in the thick waves to tilt her head back. Although still troubled, her pupils swelled as she peered up at him. She took a breath, her lips parting around it.

He leaned down to kiss her, a reassuring brush of his lips to hers, but the gesture tingled with electricity. With only a scant pause, he pressed his mouth to hers a second time, slow, tender, and deep, smiling into it when she melted against him.

When his cell phone rang, Rowan stepped away to break the kiss, skin flushed, eyes slightly glazed. "Zoe's waiting for her change."

Luke couldn't keep the grin off his face, letting it widen when she shot him a dirty look. He glanced down at his cell, cool temperatures dousing his insides. "It's Andy."

Hand on door knob, Rowan paused, shifting toward him. Concern chased the flush away.

He picked up, bracing for the worst. His insides seemed to shrivel. "Hey, Andy."

Listening to the man's familiar rambling, relief weakened his body when he caught the words he needed to hear. Luke leaned against the desk, muscles a little watery. Rowan caught his arm, fingers pressed in, fearful gaze holding his.

He disconnected a moment later and smiled down into her eyes. "Henry's on his way back. He's a tough old bird."

Chapter Twenty-Three

Marcus Ady slumped down against his sweat-stained mattress. Humidity sank its claws into him, made worse by the perpetual low-grade fever he now suffered from.

Fury ran hot through his blood, but he'd tempered it enough to crystalize and dissect his thoughts. Intense emotions could only lead to mistakes and chaos. He couldn't afford to allow it. A calm cool mind was essential.

A heavy veil had dropped, cutting off access to the girl. When he drank the potent mixture to send his mind to roam, it had bounced back, indicating someone else's protection magic.

There was no way to know whom it belonged to, but whoever did the spellcasting was powerful. Impressively so. It wasn't associated with the original protection spell, but it did build upon it.

The first had had nothing to do with Marcus, it just worked against him at the root. A very old maternal spell which attempted to protect those residing within the walls of the old building. But there had been thin areas that Marcus had been able to traverse. He'd been able to seek petty revenge on Jimmy, tormenting him on a psychological level, but the physical and the soul were lost to him. Marcus had used those gaps to stir the pot with the girl, preparing her, weakening her.

But now those holes had been plugged up, reinforced.

A fresh wave of anger had him shaking, and he pulled himself up from his makeshift bed. He reined it back in, struggling for control. His muscles were weak, but the fire of his mind coaxed them to move. He left the tiny bedroom he slept in, grabbing on to the doorjamb when he wobbled.

Pulling in a few cleansing breaths, he stepped forward to enter his altar room.

It was more than just the place he prayed and worked. It was the heart of his home, the heart of him. The locked walk-in closet contained his remaining talismans. Marcus gritted his teeth at the memory, the betrayal. Jimmy's fear and rage could have ended his long life, but the man hadn't been able destroy them all. No, not all. But their power had ebbed. It would all soon be gone, the spirit energy dissipating into nothingness. Then he would die. It was inevitable, unless he could tap into the young, bright soul of the girl. The blood soul of his enemy.

When he'd been close to her that first night, her energy hummed with vibrancy and strength. The timing only confirmed the wishes of his gods. He would continue to survive. He'd believed it to be his fate.

Now he wasn't so sure.

Marcus surveyed the storage unit where he stocked his supplies. With little pause, he pulled an old text from the second shelf. He slid to the floor, shuffling through pages of the ancient book. His memory whispered that somewhere, someway, there was a way around. He needed to find it.

As he read, his muscles stiffened beneath him, pain radiating into his bones, but he remained still, determined. Spell by spell, his own notations lining the edges, he scoured the text. He refused to let panic impede him, choosing to allow deep, even breaths to keep his mind focused.

The sun touched the horizon and his animals slid into their morning schedule. The sounds of hungry and restless livestock filtered in from the outside when Ady's solution finally emerged from the depths. Marcus sighed, rolling his head against his shoulders in an attempt to relax his bone and gristle.

Yes, the new protection magic on the girl and the tavern was solid. Someone had taken a tremendous amount of care to be sure of it.

But he wondered if that someone knew there was a way around it. Marcus allowed the smallest of smiles, suspecting how ghastly it must now look but not caring. He rarely looked in the mirror these days anyway.

There was no doubt it would take a little more time and he needed to prepare. It wouldn't be without risk. He was powerful, but magic didn't necessarily correspond to physicality. His body was weak, becoming weaker every day. The fever kept him chilled or roasting. Perspiration and tremors were constant companions. He had to believe it was all temporary. In his experience, belief was just as strong as the physical. He would hold on, and keep his wits about him. He would have to go into the city. He'd be vulnerable, but there was no choice any longer.

The alternative was unacceptable.

Chapter Twenty-Four

Rowan clamped her arms around his midsection, pressing her cheek to Luke's back as he wove the bike with expert care through city traffic. The power of the machine beneath her and the wind whipping past gave her a jubilant feeling of invincibility. It was now easy to see the appeal of traveling by motorcycle.

He leaned into the turn and guided them through the shadows of the hospital parking garage. Finding a space not far from the stairwell, Luke cut off the deep rumbling growl of the engine. He waited until she'd hopped off to follow suit.

Andy had delivered some wonderful news about Henry and Rowan felt almost as relieved as Luke looked. Over the past couple of months, she'd developed a sincere affection for her favorite customer.

The old man had a road ahead of him, but his doctor assured the family that perseverance and therapy could bring him back to himself. Or at least pretty damned close. Considering what could have occurred, they'd take it.

Luke's hand curled around hers and his lip twitched in a tiny smile. She squeezed his fingers as they made their way through the lobby, heading for the elevators. This time they wouldn't be going up to intensive care. Henry had been placed in a regular room for the interim, although depending on Andy's wishes, he'd either be transferred to a rehab center or brought home with supervision and therapy visits.

They stepped from the elevator on the fourth floor and hung a right, skirting around staff, other visitors, and the occasional wandering patient.

Henry was on his own in room 407, his family

seeing to their respective outside responsibilities. The old man appeared shriveled and pale, but he slowly turned his head when they entered. His smile drooped to the left, but it reached the warm brown of his eyes.

"What's this? It's not like you to be laying around, Henry." Luke had gripped Rowan's hand in startled response, but his voice remained steady in playful mockery. "Unless you've got some cute nurses. Then I suppose I might be able to excuse it."

"Some … always pleasant … but I'd prefer to be … drinking with … the boys…" The man's words were slow and slurred. Saliva glinted on his chin.

Rowan stepped forward, grabbed a tissue off the bedside table, and gently wiped his mouth. She smiled. "Hi, Henry."

Embarrassment etched into his face, and Rowan touched his arm, speaking softly. "You'll be back soon. Your stool is waiting for you. We won't let anyone else sit there. Your boys wrapped some caution tape around it."

"Really?" The old man looked beyond her, fixed on Luke, who nodded.

It was true. The day of Henry's stroke, the other regulars marked the stool as off-limits.

"Good … to know. I'll … have to get … bett … er faster … now." He spoke with some effort, enunciating and drawing out each word.

"You do that."

Luke stepped behind Rowan, casually resting his hands on her shoulders. Henry raised his brows in pleasure and amusement. "I'm out … of it … for a lit-tle while … and you … two stubborn asses … find one … another. Je suis content pour toi. I'm hap-py for you."

Her insides jittered a little at the old man's observation. Unsure how to react, she chose not to, deciding to take an impulsive leap instead. "Henry, may I ask you something? It concerns my uncle."

He frowned, fatigue reverberating through his crinkled features. "Of course, ma chère."

Guilt sliced through her the moment the words left her mouth. The man was exhausted. A tiny string of saliva escaped his drooping mouth a second time and Rowan wiped it away. "Never mind. You should get some rest."

Henry's brown eyes locked on hers. "That's all I'm ... doin' in here ... resting ... unless the thera-pists come in to ... torture me. What you ... want to ... know?"

Rowan hesitated. She didn't know how likely it was that Jimmy would have confided in Henry when he hadn't felt compelled to talk to Luke. Even as Henry watched in expectation, she knew she should never have even brought it up. It was selfish and stupid. He didn't need to be saddled with her issues as he recovered from a stroke. Shame burned her face and she stared down at the toes of her flats.

"La Jeune fille ne peut pas parler?"

Luke shook his head and nudged one visitor chair over to Rowan. He grabbed the second one and perched on the edge. Silence hung between them while she debated.

"Ask ... me." His gaze flickered between the two of them. "Is it some ... thing to do with ... his illness?"

"You knew about that?"

"Oui. He was in ... pain for long time. Got ... so much worse. Miser-able. Nothing seemed ... to help." What little color he had faded from his cheeks. His eyelids sagged, struggled to open. "Then ... something ... did."

Her heart blasted in her ears, but she waited.

Luke's hand squeezed her shoulder, relaxed.

"He started going … to one of … those places. Well, wasn't … even a shop he said … some … house. Desperate, I think." Henry's shaking hand found hers. "I was afraid … for him … told him to stay a-way. Said those avenues could … bring … bad juju."

"I know he didn't listen, Henry." Rowan folded the old man's hand between both of hers. "What do you mean by bad 'juju'? Wasn't he looking for some kind of drug?"

"Maybe." The old man blinked, unease flickering before sadness coated his face like a pasty film. "Your uncle …he stubborn."

"It seems to run in the family," Luke remarked, and Rowan shot him an unimpressed look over her shoulder. He lowered his voice. "He didn't talk to me about any of this."

"Did he happen to tell you where he went for help?"

"Little. Said he was … going down around … Second Street. Laughed, kind of … nervous though. Not a good … area. Told me … to … wish him luck…"

Luke growled and Rowan turned to look at him. His jaw pulsed and steel glinted in his eyes. Compassion reared up inside her. Luke didn't trust easily and Jimmy had betrayed him by simple omission.

"Stopped … talking to … me about … things. I bring it up … when he seemed to hurt … less. Said he … found … something that works." Henry shook his head. It seemed too heavy for him and he stopped. "Drug or spell, I don't … know but he was happy, or at least he wasn't in pain. Then things … went bad…"

"Spell?"

"Don't know … hard to say. I don't have … much … exper-i-ence with that stuff." The way his eyes

185

darted, Rowan figured he knew more about that world than what he cared to admit.

"Son of a bitch. If he'd only—" Luke stopped, rested his hands atop his head, and stared toward the window. Full clouds pushed against a brilliant slash of blue sky.

Henry looked at both of them, his brows pulling together. "Why is this … coming up … now? Jimmy's long gone. Is there some-thing else … going … on?"

"No." Rowan shook her head, the lie burning her throat. "I've been trying to piece that last year together. From all the bits I've heard, everything just seems so pretty unbelievable." Leaning forward, she met his eyes. "If you knew who he went to see, you would tell us, wouldn't you, Henry? You wouldn't be afraid?"

He went quiet, gazing down at the hand in his. With a small sigh, he nodded. "If he got in-to what … I think he did … yes, I would be a-fraid. My mama didn't … raise idiots, but yes, I also would tell … you."
                    ****

"I feel like complete crap." Rowan pressed the down button on the elevator with more ferocity than necessary. "Poor old guy stared down the tunnel at death, came back, and here I am pumping him for information."

"You have a right to know, Rowan. Henry understands that."

"Does he? As far as he's concerned, I'm beating a dead horse."

The doors slid open and they stepped inside. "I'll let Dave know about the Second Street thing. I doubt anything will come of it, but you never know."

Rowan leaned against the wall of the elevator, hands hooked on the railing behind her. "The not knowing is going to drive me off my nut. If he comes for me, well, that scares the crap out of me, but at least that should end it. Otherwise, I just continue to live my life with this shadow over me. He might pop up. He might crawl off and die and I'd never know. How long do I have to live like this?"

She raised her big gray eyes to him, angry but beseeching. When he tried to wrap an arm around her, she sidestepped away. "I'm not sure you should even do that anymore."

"What are you talking about?"

A grim smile sliced across her features. "Marked woman here. May not live to see her twenty-ninth birthday. Probably not worth the investment."

Dark and insidious anger coursed through his veins, and before he realized what he was doing, he smacked the stop button and cornered her with his body. Ignoring the shock on her face, he leaned in, a low growl rumbling from within. "Don't even think that, let alone say it. I've already determined you're worth the investment. Whether or not that stays true is between you and me only, not some second-rate freak masquerading as a nightmare. Got it?"

Rowan stared up at him, misty eyes sparking, then thawing. Her sweet breath reached him and on an inward groan, he took her mouth with his, aggressive enough to make his point. When he pulled away, he ran a gentle hand over her hair and repeated himself. "Got it?"

She continued to gaze at him, eyes darkened to charcoal, lips slightly swollen. "Fair enough. Don't say I didn't warn you though."

"Duly noted." He released the stop button. "Now for tonight I had a suggestion."

"I bet."

Luke tilted his head, sending her a side look. "Get your mind out of the gutter. I was thinking pizza and some videos."

NANCY E. POLIN

"I guess I could be down with that."

Chapter Twenty-Five

"That was evil." Rowan huffed from her corner of the couch.

"C'mon, it was fun."

"You're idea of fun is seriously warped." She folded her arms across her breasts. "I'll have you know it almost got me disowned."

"Any parent who would disown their kid for something like that has a serious stick up their ass."

She shook her head, keeping her face still for as long as possible. But after a few moments, she couldn't help herself. There was no more holding back. All her current darkness fell aside and giggles erupted into laughter that had tears squirting from her eyes. "You … you should have seen my mother's face! I mean, I did warn her, but once she's determined to do something, there's no getting in her way."

"What? She didn't think Night of the Bloody Hand was Oscar bait? Man, how narrow-minded."

Rowan snorted, wiping her eyes. Leaning forward, she snagged her can of cola off the coffee table and took a swig. "When I decided to leave school to pursue the Hollywood dream, she didn't speak to me for three weeks. My father was a little better about it, but he tended to side with my mom. Just easier for him since he lived under the same roof. Didn't keep him from calling me from his office, though. When I actually landed a small guest part in a pretty well-received television series, she came around a little, started bragging to her friends. And then that was it. The next part was in Terror Island and then there was this one." She shrugged, thinking back with bittersweet amusement. "I guess I wasn't destined beyond C-grade."

"And your mom never forgave you."

"Not really, but she softened a bit after—"
Stopping, she took a breath. Oddly enough, it didn't hurt any longer. It just irritated her.

"What?"

"After I caught my fiancée boffing my former best friend." She shrugged and took another sip of her drink.

Luke frowned and took a pull of his beer. "Sounds like a real fuckwad."

"Yeah, he was. At least I found out before I married him." She rubbed a thumb through the condensation on the soda can. "Afterward, my mom dropped by, gave me a hug and told me I should have expected it from that type of person."

"What type was that?"

"Actor."

"Oh."

"Like me." She allowed a closed-mouth smile. "She always knows the right thing to say."

Luke smirked and shifted toward her to run one finger down her thigh. "I'm sure your mother would love me. I mean, I may not be an actor, but I do ride a motorcycle."

Rowan chuckled. "You have no idea. Anyway, not long after that, we got news of my uncle's passing and the even weirder news that he'd left me this place. I suppose I took it as a sign it was time to move on."

"Done with acting?"

"Yeah. It was fun, crazy, annoying, hard, occasionally interesting, but it's not for me."

"I'm sure your mother's delighted."

Giggles threatened to return and she pressed the back of her hand to her mouth. "Um, yeah. Owning a bar is so much better."

He gazed at her, eyes shining, soft and amused. After several beats of silence, she squirmed, uncomfortable. "What?"

Reaching over, he brushed her hair behind one ear, seemed to contemplate saying something, but pulled her to him instead. He pressed his lips to her brow, cheek, and mouth.

Opening herself up, physically and emotionally, she welcomed him.

****

Rowan curled into him, one leg looped over his and head resting in the crook of his shoulder. She caressed his chest with one hand, exploring the sculpted planes of muscle from his smooth side to his damaged side. She ignored his sudden intake of breath, knowing it was instinctive, and continued the movement. Keeping her voice at a whisper, she forced herself to ask the questions she'd wanted to ask since the first time she'd seen him shirtless. "Will you tell me about yourself, Luke? Your past? Will you tell me what happened?"

He let out a long sigh. "You want to know my life story?"

"It would be nice. For the most part, you know about me."

His body tensed for a long moment, then relaxed, resigned. "It's been quite a few years, but it's still hard to talk about it."

"I'm sorry."

He brushed a kiss to the crown of her head. "I hate feeling vulnerable."

"Says the naked guy."

A chuckle vibrated through his chest, but when she glanced up at him, the strain weathered his face into that of an older man. Sorrow for him stole any attempt to lighten the moment. "Never mind, Luke. You don't have to tell me if you're not ready, or you just don't want to."

Saying nothing, he ran one hand lightly up and down her back, but the tension in his body didn't waver. She listened to his breathing and the beat of his heart, startling when he finally began to speak.

"You want to know everything? Every little detail that resulted in the fucked-up man you're cozying up with? Are you sure?" Bitterness sifted through his voice.

"Yes, but I'll settle for whatever you're willing to share." She nestled closer, holding on in an attempt to let him know she didn't plan on going anywhere.

Luke sighed and brushed a kiss to her hair. "All right. I guess it's only fair."
****

He pulled in a deep breath and decided to let her in. It was time.

"My father died when I was two and my mother couldn't be what a little kid needed. High strung, nervous, kind of sickly. My older sister flew under the radar, but I got caught in the crossfire most of the time. My stepfather spent a lot of time placating my mom, keeping things quiet, so a rambunctious young boy was a thorn in his side. During the school year, I was shuttled off to daycare until they closed, then brought home, fed and sent to bed. That's how my grandmother wound up raising me for the most part. Every summer, every school vacation, hell, every teacher-in-service day, I was sent off to stay with her."

"That's awful."

"Nah, it was actually okay." He shook his head in memory. "My parents couldn't handle me, but grand-mere, she was tough. Tough, fair, kind, loving. What I needed. Growing up, I wanted to make her proud of me even when she threatened to box my ears." He managed a low laugh. "She reined me in, helped me to focus, helped me over my anger at being, in my perspective, abandoned by my parents. As I grew older, I began to realize my mother was heavily flawed, even mentally ill. I don't think she ever got over losing my father, and George, my step, was, is, a low-level replacement. They couldn't have helped me. But, my grand-mere, she set me down the right path, enough that I went to college, even spent the summer after graduation working at a pub in Ireland. Hell, maybe that was a little life foreshadowing for me.

"When I got home, I lost direction again. I'd majored in sociology in college and didn't have a clue what to do with it. Nothing sounded intriguing enough to pursue, plus I would have had to go back to school for additional degrees to even make it worth my while. So that was that. I bummed around for a while, taking odd jobs … worked at a beverage manufacturer cleaning tanks, did some paint mixing at this auto place, um, worked at a sawmill, I built fences, did some carpentry, in general, did lots of crap work. Then I was having a beer with some guys after my shift when a couple firefighters came in. That moment I had that little-kid epiphany." Luke smiled down at her, but it looked strained. "I decided to be a fireman when I grew up.

"I applied, went through all the interviewing, physicals, passed the test, and actually got in as a recruit. Grand-mere was so excited for me. Hell, even my mother and stepdad crawled out from their hole to wish me well.

"Went through all the training in Baton Rouge, came back here. The night before I was to report to my house, I went back to that same bar for a quiet drink on my own … and that's when I met Catherine. She was working there, here, a few nights a week to pay her way through college."

"Your wife worked for Jimmy?"

Luke closed his eyes and took a breath. Discomfort ached inside. "Yeah, she did."

Her eyes remained fastened to him, soft and compassionate. "You okay?"

"I think now that I've started, I should go ahead and get it all out. Maybe I'll just fast forward a bit though." His tried to smile. "Like pulling off a Band-Aid."

"All right."

"We hit it off. I mean, she was beautiful inside and out. She balanced me and was everything I ever wanted. We slipped off and got married six months later. Probably on the fast side, but we were so sure. A year after that, McKenzie was born." He paused, but shook his head. "I haven't spoken of it for years. I guess it's time.

"I'd just gotten off shift and was heading home. We'd had a couple of calls during the night, so I was ready to drop over. The plan was a good night's sleep, then take my girls to the zoo... McKenzie wanted to see the white alligator ... she was at that age where all animals were fascinating." Luke huffed another smile in memory, but his eyes stung. He cleared his throat. "Bosco, um, Cate's cat, would run whenever he saw the baby coming. She was pretty gentle most of the time, but once in a while ... well, that was all it took for the cat to avoid her."

Tears slid down Rowan's cheeks in silence, their wetness spilling against his chest.

"A couple of blocks from the house, my own company blew right past me. I'm not sure how I knew ... or maybe I didn't ... I don't know. I just hit it, had this wild urge to get home. It happens after a particularly difficult shift. That's what I told myself. But when I got there, my house, our house, was ... engulfed. I stood there like an idiot and then proceeded to forget every bit of training I'd ever had. Completely blanked. All I knew was I had to get to Cate and Kenzie. A couple of the guys tried to stop me, but I broke a nose … I'm not even sure whose anymore … and got past them. It was suffocating in there. I could feel the hair on my arms burning. It's hard to remember much after that. Most of it's just what I was told. The roof collapsed when a couple of the guys were pulling me out. Someone said I was on fire … when I woke up later, I found out they hadn't been bullshitting me."

The late hour socked in around them, broken only by the distant sound of traffic.

Rowan held on, pressing her face to his chest, and his arms tightened around her.

"Cause of the fire was faulty wiring. We'd just bought the house seven or eight months before, too. Cate said it was perfect. Small enough to be cozy, big enough to grow. We were even trying for another baby."

"I'm so very sorry, Luke. It's not enough though. I'm not really sure what to say." Her voice shook, but warmth flowed through him at her struggle. Her compassion settled over him, giving, comfortable.

"It's okay. No one else knew either. I was in the hospital for too damned long, had nowhere to go when I got out. Grand-mere had died the year before. I couldn't go to my mother. My sister was, is, in fucking Ohio and there was no way I'd land on her doorstep anyway. She has enough on her plate."

"Jimmy gave you a place to stay."

Luke nodded, squeezed his eyes shut for a moment. "Even if I wanted to go back to work … from a psychological perspective, I couldn't. That part of my life is over. Since then, it's fair to say I've been using this place to hide. Just getting to the point that I can admit that."

He tilted his head to catch her eye. "At least to you, Rowan."

Eyes still wet, she touched his cheek and then inched up to brush his lips with hers.

He shifted to wrap his arms more tightly around her and kiss her tears away. Awareness thrummed deep inside, emotions surging, sharpening. Despite all his pain, all his admissions, he wanted to comfort this beautiful, compassionate woman nestled within his arms. He couldn't stand to see her cry, even if was over his own personal hell.

Maybe, just maybe, it was a sign he was finally healing.

Chapter Twenty-Six

Rowan unconsciously twisted the gris-gris between the fingers of one pocketed hand as more of a comfort thing than anything else. She watched the crowds, an amused smile resting against her face. Folks really went above and beyond for the holiday and as an avid people watcher, it was a treat for her.

She and Luke had left Christy in charge at the tavern to head out for a little Halloween fun. After weeks of looking over her shoulder, she finally started to relax. Nothing had come of Henry's tip about Second Street, but there'd been no hallucinations or nightmares since Ruth had cast her protection spells either. Rowan couldn't help but wonder if the man was now dead or at least too weak to pursue her. As dark and disturbing as the thought was, she hoped for the former, unsure what that said about her. Luke would point out that it was a normal reaction. Whether it was or not, she chose not to analyze it. At least not tonight.

They'd hiked down to Decatur Street to check out the annual Halloween parade. Riding on imaginatively demented floats and in dune buggies, costumed people high on life and alcohol threw treats and small gifts out to the crowds. Rowan came away with handfuls of candy and one strand of glimmering beads, courtesy of an impressive dive catch of Luke's and not an inappropriate flash from her. Afterward, they'd been sucked into the energy of the city and wandered the streets to land at an autumn carnival.

Luke stood in line for drinks a few short feet away and her insides took a quick dip and warmed. Her heart ached whenever she thought of his loss, but she was thrilled he trusted her enough to open up. The man he'd pretended to be versus the man he revealed little by little was very different. His gradual revelation was not unlike peeling away layers of paint to find original beauty underneath. It made her head spin when she contemplated it.

Gazing at him, she traced his face, now knowing how those hard lines could soften into unexpected tenderness when he held her close. Also knowing how they could still freeze in temper or annoyance. A steady thrum pulsed in her lower belly and heat spread out in enticing threads. Everything had become a little too clear. Her feelings for him had taken a long and twisted road but the destination had turned inevitable. She thought back to their first meeting a few months earlier and shook her head in amazement and quiet resignation.

A costumed devil knocked into her and continued to stagger past. Gasping in surprise, she stumbled back a step, catching herself before she fell. Something in the man's costume was honed to a sharpened edge, and Rowan felt the sting and burn. She snatched her hand away, frowning down at the small trickle of blood on the webbing between her thumb and forefinger.

Luke appeared next to her, shoving a drink served in a plastic grenade toward her. "I had to battle an Ork, Sasquatch, and an undead colonial soldier for that, so I figure it's got to be good." He took a swig of his own to demonstrate before taking a closer look at her. His dark brows crinkled. "What's the matter?"

"Nothing … some drunk almost knocked me over. His costume had a sharp edge or something. It's not a big deal." She flexed her hand and he took it in his.

"Just a scratch, but I'll take care of it when we get back." He smiled at her and her heart did a quick skip. She was still getting used to how beautiful his smiles were.

They delved into the crowd, sliding into the beat of a local band. A few carnival rides spread out to her right and she pulled him toward the Ferris wheel. He stopped and frowned as he stared up at it.

"Scared?" She bumped her hip into his.

"Not exactly. Just wondering how many bolts were left behind when it was last set up."

"Well, there's a cheery thought." Her fingers curled around his. "Let's live dangerously."

Rowan laughed at his grim expression, but he followed her, reconciled to his fate.

From the top, the view pulled in all the lights of the city. In the distance, they could see a riverboat paddling its way down the Mississippi and Rowan thought about that day she was down by the dock, contemplating a cruise on her own. Now she sensed Luke might be willing to join her. Content, she leaned against him and his arm looped over her shoulders, his lips brushing the top of her head. Smiling, she angled her head up toward him and he took the hint, laying his lips against hers.

****

Luke sighed, aware of a new sense of peace burgeoning inside. He tried not to contemplate it, fearing it would disappear as quickly as it had settled in. He caressed her cheek and smiled as she pressed her face into his hand. Maybe everything would actually work out. Ruth's protection spells seemed to have warded off advances of the bokor. He could only hope it stayed that way. The old woman was powerful and any other priest would be aware of it.

As the ride made its rotation, in one swift move, Rowan flipped over to straddle him. He felt his jaw sag as a bolt of heat and lust shot through his bloodstream along with sincere shock. She pressed against him and he couldn't bite back the groan. "What … what are you doing?"

"Isn't that obvious?" She slid her body over his. "How's this for living dangerously?"

Confused, he threaded his hand into her hair, holding her head still to look into her eyes. "Rowan?"

Her smoky eyes glinted silver in the artificial light. "Luke." She leaned in, molding her mouth to his aggressively, one hand venturing to stroke him through his jeans. "What's the matter? I could give you a little ride within the ride." She bit his neck and he startled.

Grabbing her shoulders, he pushed her away enough to stare into her face.

She grinned and ran her tongue over her teeth. "What's the matter? Don't you want to fuck?"

"What? As much as the prospect appeals, I don't think the here and now is the best choice." Luke frowned, alarms blaring within the confines of his skull. What began as a surprising, but exciting, little twist now had all his senses on full alert.

"Oh, come on." She groped him none too gently. He grunted and clenched his teeth. "Your body is telling me something different than your words."

"What the hell's the matter with you?" Heartbeat thudding from lust to fear, he held her tight, trying to read her face.

"What the hell's the matter with you? I thought all guys—" Her words tumbled to a stop, eyes widening in shock. She stared at him, bewilderment pushing out lust like the turn of a page. "Luke, I … I don't feel well…"

Every ounce of color bled from her face as her fingers gripped his forearms before loosening. Her eyes rolled backward and she slumped.

He caught her before she could sink to the bottom

of the pod, hugging her to him. His heart thundered hard enough to bruise his ribs when the sudden scorching fever heat of her body bled against his.

Luke yelled for the operator to stop the ride, but it took two complete cycles for the wheel to come to a halt. By that time, she'd come around, blinking up at him in confusion, the flare of fever gone.

"Let's get you to the hospital." He tried to lift her, but she pushed against him, shaking her head. Fear chilled him as he watched her wobble a little and he darkly wondered if he was destined to lose Rowan, too, shaking it off a moment later.

No, that couldn't happen. No fucking way.

****

A little unsteady, strength gradually flowed back into her muscles. "I'm okay." The words sounded hollow to her own ears, so she tried again. "Really, Luke. I'm okay. I think I just want to go."

He stared at her, dubious.

"Please." She touched his cheek. "Please."

The ride operator shifted his substantial weight from foot to foot. "She okay?"

"I'm fine." Rowan didn't know if she was or not. Her body tingled as if she'd received one hell of an electric shock and snippets of humiliating memories warmed her face. White-hot lust had boiled her blood, and in those moments, she'd wanted him any way she could get him inside her.

That hadn't been her. Had it? The idea of such a public display was unfathomable. Their rainy day embrace had been bad enough.

Luke wrapped an arm around her waist. "All right, let's get out of here."

She nodded. "I'm so sorry, Luke."

A half-smile pulled at his face. "Don't be. You

surprised me, that's all. And then scared off a few years of life. Good thing I'm relatively young."

Troubled, she didn't smile.

Luke guided her through the crowd, using himself as a battering ram when necessary, earning multiple oaths and one bird in his direction. She leaned into him, hoping to absorb some of his strength. God, she hated feeling vulnerable.

The throng of people gradually disappeared and she let out a relieved sigh. At least they weren't all that far away from home. Home. She almost smiled at the thought.

"Did you want to grab some late dinner?" He squeezed her hand. "Protein might help."

Rowan considered the suggestion for a moment before nodding. Despite her episode, or whatever the hell it was, she'd been enjoying her time out with him. "Um, sure. That's probably a good idea."

They stopped at a popular local place that actively shooed out the under-twenty-one set with the presence of poker machines. Weathered brick, open beams, ceiling fans, and subdued lighting gave the place a pleasant, rustic feel.

They claimed a corner table on the perimeter where they could relax and watch the dance and prance of the intoxicated close to the bar. Rowan reached across the table to curl her fingers with his and he brushed his thumb over the silkiness of her skin. The cut had dried, leaving a crusting of blood over the small wound. A purplish bruise spread out from either side. "You should go wash that."

She gazed down at it, puzzled. "Oh, I guess I'd forgotten." Pushing away from the table, she threw him a tiny smile and wandered through the crowd toward the back hallway, pushing through the swinging door into the ladies room.

Several other women clamored at the mirror, but she located the one free sink at the end, using the medicinal-smelling soap to clean the cut. It was just a narrow slash, but it pulsed more than it seemed to have a right to.

When she heard the whisper, she glanced over and frowned. "I'm sorry?"

The woman next to her attended to a complex series of eye shadow layers, face tense in concentration. She paused to shoot Rowan a narrow look. "What?"

"I'm sorry. I thought you said something."

"Wasn't me. Maybe the little people at the bottom of the bottle are talking to you." She guffawed at her own joke and went back to layer number six.

A low roar built in Rowan's ears, the whisper shielded within. She shook her head and stared into her own eyes. Dots blotted out the reflection and she blinked repeatedly until they cleared.

She wondered when the hell she'd developed tinnitus. Wasn't that what ringing in the ears was?

The whisper threaded through her head again, but she couldn't decipher the words. They sounded alien, muddled, and unrecognizable. She glanced over where several other women washed hands, brushed hair, touched up makeup. None acted as if anything were awry.

Disquiet crept up the back of her neck, bringing the chill of sweat, and she pulled in a deep, steadying breath.

Cupping her hands under the spigot, she brought them to her face, closing her eyes as the cool water ran down her heated skin. She repeated the motion several times before blotting with paper towels.

The whispers eased and her mind erased them.

She slid back out into the bar, gaze zeroing in on Luke. He'd ordered her a hurricane and himself a beer, taking a swig as she gazed at him. She watched his hands, loving the strength of them, knowing what pleasures they were capable of inducing. The thought fluttered around the primal part of her brain and Rowan's cheeks heated. She was thankful for the dim light.

It was so much more now.

The physical was lovely, but there were times when she felt like she was falling, despite knowing her feet were firm against the earth. Her brain would become muddled for a long moment before clarifying into that beautiful and coveted emotion. A connection, contentious at the beginning, had turned into something so much bigger than she could have ever imagined. She'd thought she'd loved Craig, but compared to what wove around her heart now, it seemed like a distant second-grade crush.

She allowed herself to observe him a few more moments, distantly noting the slide of something insidious weaving with her warm feelings just beneath the flesh. Shaking her head to dispel it, she returned to her seat.

****

"Better?" Luke stood when she appeared back at the table.

"Mmm hmm."

The waiter swooped by to collect their orders and Luke shot up an eyebrow when Rowan ordered a hefty portion of fried chicken with all the trimmings, but shrugged a second later. He'd probably get to sample when she only finished half. When he ordered his own meal, he landed on the other end of a scowl.

"Rabbit jambalaya?"

"What? It's delicious."

"Bunny. You're going to eat a bunny."

"Yummy." He grinned, winked, and sipped his beer. Much better. Her fire and color were back. Luke gave an inward sigh of relief, unwilling to admit how much the incident on the Ferris wheel had shaken him. His lizard brain naturally wanted to consider a new exciting layer to the woman, while his logical side slapped him around and told him to stop thinking with his penis.

Nonetheless, he observed her carefully without allowing it to appear she was being scrutinized. If nothing, he was excellent at feigning indifference.

She chatted about future plans for The Goose, mentioned an obligatory trip back to L.A. to see her parents, and even managed to leech a little more information about his own family from him. Nothing about the past couple of months surfaced.

It was business as usual and Luke began to relax.

When the waiter arrived with their meals, he bit into a forkful of his jambalaya, enjoying the spice and mélange of flavors, frowning a moment later at Rowan. She'd torn into her food, eating with an exuberance he'd never witnessed from her before. An uneasy thought brought on by memory of another woman and another time brought a cool clamminess to his skin.

Cate had eaten like that before finding out she was pregnant with McKenzie.

Nausea clenched his belly and he reached for his beer, finishing it in a couple large gulps. That couldn't be. They'd been careful. For the most part. Images of an impulsive afterhours tumble behind the bar introduced chips of ice into his blood.

No way.

Probably a natural bodily reaction to her earlier weakness. It would stand to reason that all that stress and reduced appetite would culminate in such a response. That was it. It made sense.

"Are you okay?" Rowan stared at him, pausing with a hush puppy halfway to her mouth. "You look a little pale."

He cleared his throat, wanting water, flagging down the waiter for some. "I'm fine, just worried about you."

"No need." The two words came out around her food and Luke winced. Her table manners appeared to have taken a hiatus. "I feel good. Really good."

As if just remembering, she swallowed and wiped her mouth with a paper napkin.

"You've certainly discovered your appetite."

She grimaced and glanced down at her dinner before meeting his gaze with a slow, wanton smile that made his heart lurch and all his thoughts disintegrate. "Maybe I need the energy for later."

Chapter Twenty-Seven

Rowan didn't quite understand what was happening.

She felt giddy before they'd left the restaurant and it still permeated by the time they reached The Goose. Even the choice to walk hadn't suppressed it. Now as they approached the bustle of the tavern, she was too aware of each point of contact with Luke. Their fingers stayed entwined, palms pressed together. Occasionally, they'd bump against one another or he'd pull her close to make some kind of witty observation in a dry tone that had her bursting with laughter.

The moment they stepped inside, Justin lifted a hand in a greeting that didn't reach his eyes and Christy smiled as she buzzed by with a tray. But Rowan could only manage to acknowledge them on the most cursory of levels. Something else reared up, heating her, making her pound from within. Sweat dampened her forehead, muscles tensing, and she squeezed Luke's hand a second before giving it a strong yank.

He looked down at her, one brow lifting in question.

Despite the tremors growing stronger from within, she took a deep breath and smiled at him. She needed to step back before the fire consumed her from within, but patience was something difficult to maintain.

She needed him. Now.

And it confused the hell out of her. Not that she didn't want him, no that wasn't it. The very act of looking at him was enough to have her hormones humming, but the current power of her need overwhelmed her.

Control waning, Rowan pressed close, one arm

around his waist, the other hand curled in the fabric of his shirt. As they walked, her fingers poked beneath, stroking the lean muscles of his stomach above the waistband and evoking a shudder from him.

The moment they stepped into the little apartment, she pulled him down to her, blistering his lips with a hard, intense kiss. His body melded with hers as he wrapped his arms around her, one hand cradling the back of her head, the other splayed across her hip. Her aggression seemed to kindle his own, swelling with a demanding excitement.

When he lifted her, she wrapped her legs around his waist, and he stumbled into the bedroom, dropping her onto the mattress and following her down.

Luke sought to roll her beneath him, but she pushed back, reversing their positions until she grinned down into his face. Tipping forward, she caught his lower lip between her teeth to give it a playful tug, joining her mouth with his the moment after to ease the sting of her nip.

She wanted him at her mercy, something sensual, yet dark and malignant flaring deep inside at the thought. Her body hummed with intensity, fear from the evening shrinking from memory.

****

Unwilling to give her complete control, he cradled her face to return the kiss, holding tight as if she were mist ready to slip between his fingers. The light floral scent of her filled him, fuzzing his brain but heating his blood and flesh. His need and want boiled over when she pressed her body flush to his. When he tried to flip her over once more, she broke the kiss and pulled away, flashing a grin that reminded him of something feral, dangerous. The gray of her eyes glinted like a knife's blade and a flutter of unease seesawed inside him for the second time that night.

"No, you don't."

When fabric ripped and buttons of his shirt popped, the ominous feeling escaped him. She pushed his clothing aside to run her hands over his chest, replacing them with her mouth. She bit his shoulder, laving and kissing her way across his torso. There was no pause over his scars. Rowan accepted his damage without hesitation. Fire ignited his blood and loins as Luke pulled her up to cover her mouth with his. She returned it, deeply, yanked away, and shoved him back into the pillows to explore his body with her hands, nails, and mouth. A long groan rattled from between his lips, but he watched her intently.

Unzipping him, she stroked and caressed, at once gentle but building, soon skirting the line of roughness. He jerked with a grunt, and she grinned up at him, eyes bright.

"Rowan…"

"Shhh … relax. Let me make you feel good."

She slowly built him up again, using fingers, hands, teeth, and lips. Tortured, his breath whooshed deafeningly in his ears, his heart slamming itself to jagged pieces against his ribcage. When Rowan backed off, Luke belly-growled, blood pressure ready to erupt. He made a grab for her, but she slipped past, laughing. The sound was low and sultry, winding him up even more.

Did she want him to cry? It certainly felt like it.

Returning to him, she leaned down to press her lips to his, at once soft and tender, a perfect contradiction to her earlier roughness. She settled over him, her body tightening around him, and a long moan escaped his lips. When he opened his eyes, he found her gazing down at him, her gray eyes alight with mischief, but as he watched, they shifted. Desire turned them graphite, but something else shone from deep inside. Something he was afraid to see, acknowledge, despite his own solidifying emotions.

Her movements were slow, teasing once more, her gaze not leaving his. She rested her hands against his chest for balance, squeezing his hips with her thighs. When she stopped, her brows drew together, mouth parting as if she wanted to say something. Her lips pressed together, the moment passing, and Luke couldn't stand it any longer.

Flipping her around, he buried his face in her hair even as he drove himself into her. Every pretense of control vanished, and a gasp, followed by a low mewl, sounded in his ear. Rowan clung to him, keeping up even as her body quaked with release.

Sweat dampened his skin, his heart and breathing continuing to roar. Dimly aware of tears against his face, he faltered to kiss them away. Her sigh and the press of her lips to his incited him to heighten her senses, strive for her completion. Only after he'd pushed her over the brink a second time did he allow himself to follow.

He cuddled her close, kissing her perspiring brow, relishing their nearness. When he felt her body relax in slumber, Luke weighed everything within. He'd never considered he could reach this point with another woman. For years it seemed impossible, but now, as he gazed down at Rowan, the sweep of her shimmering red hair covering half of his chest, he wondered if he'd unconsciously permitted life to begin again.

And he wasn't sure if he should be grateful or terrified.

****

Luke blinked hard, trying to focus on her shadow as she moved around the room. Confusion addled his brain, and he turned to squint at the clock beside him.

2:57 glowed back at him.

"Rowan?" His voice felt gravelly, mind still murky with sleep. "Is everything all right?"

The shadow stilled as if he'd startled her and only through the scratching of instinct at the base of his brain did it occur to him that everything was definitely not all right. He rolled quickly at the sudden attack but not enough to avoid the blow. A flare of intense pain shot across the side of his head, setting off a popping of bright lights within his field of vision as he hit the carpet. When they faded, he dimly watched through cracked eyes as the small shadow went about its business as if nothing had occurred. Shock and terror for Rowan coursed through him before the roll of darkness pulled him into oblivion.

****

With movements not her own, she dropped the flashlight and finished dressing, pulling on previously laced sneakers in addition to the jeans and hoodie she'd already donned. Shaking, she wanted to go to Luke, but her body wouldn't obey. Her mind begged, pleaded for him not to be dead.

Scalding tears erupted from her eyes as she stepped over him and slid through the darkness, trying to fight the mechanical contractions of her muscles. Any screaming she might have done was buried under the heavy suffocation of her will.

Roses wafted around her at the top of the staircase, cooling into biting cold when she pushed through. She silently cried for help, and thought she felt, for the briefest of instances, a light comforting stroke across her cheek, and then nothing.

Descending the steps, her head whipped from side to side, the portal of her eyes wary despite her personal knowledge that other than Luke, no other living human currently existed within the tavern. Her body stopped short at the barricade of chairs and tables before the front door. Two more barstools slid across the worn floor as she watched, and a growl not her own rose from her chest.

Checking the heavy metal backdoor, she found it buried under an avalanche of janitorial supplies and metal shelving.

Pivoting, she headed to the kitchen and pulled a rarely used cast-iron skillet from a lower cupboard and a towel from an adjacent drawer. With jerky, restrained movements, she climbed atop the counter and slammed the cookware into one of the narrow windows above, shattering the glass with ease.

The sudden gust of frigid, otherworldly wind struck her in the face and she bent forward, narrowing her eyes against it. Using the towel, she pushed away residual glass from the frame before pulling herself up to wriggle through the small opening. Even as small as she was, it was a struggle, her body bruised and scraped by the time she was forced through. Rowan landed in a heap on the other side, protecting her head but rapping her shoulder and hip against broken macadam.

Eyes blurry with tears of fear and pain, she pushed to her feet, shoes making little sound against the deep silence of a sleeping neighborhood. Somewhere west of her, the low roar of Bourbon Street met her ears, but the lurid dissonance was much too far to help her. Muscles heavy and numb, she walked toward the next block, head fixed straight ahead. She plodded from shadow to streetlight and back again.

The old SUV was parked a few yards beyond the intersection, and as she approached, the driver leaned over and shoved open the passenger door.

When she climbed in, she didn't want to look at him, tried to keep from doing so, but she was unable. As if someone had grasped her chin and jerked her head, she found herself staring at Marcus Ady.

Brilliant, unblinking green eyes looked back at her from hollowed sockets. Crumpled, sagging skin hung from a face ravaged by disease, and ill-fitting clothes billowed around a weak frame. When he smiled, the scream inside her head was deafening, but not a sound passed from between her still lips.

He reached over to fasten her seatbelt. "Can't have you damaged. We have to leave the city."

She continued to watch him, body trembling and blood racing in heated panic. He pulled from the curb and she envisioned herself flinging the door upon and tumbling out before the truck could pick up speed. Despite the pandemonium in her head, Rowan's body continued to betray her, her hands resting boneless in her lap.

"Interesting side effects, don't you think? I hope you enjoyed yourself. You and Mr. Meunier … well, initially at least. You should have seen how the drug affected my goats." The man laughed heartedly in the dark and then his voice went matter of fact. He shrugged. "The thing about sex is it makes a man vulnerable."

He let the comment hang and Rowan closed her eyes, anguish razor sharp and biting before pure rage filled her. This man had infused himself within the physical act of her love for Luke, tainting it with his own nefarious motives.

Sweating with effort, she used that anger to push outward, finding hope when she managed to clench her fists, even weakly. They tingled and ached with the ferocity of awakening nerves. Surprised, she cut the driver a peripheral glance, trying to deduce if he'd noticed. His gaze pressed straight ahead, concentrating on guiding the SUV through the city and onto the interstate.

Channeling her fear and rage, she focused on slowly bringing her body under her own control.

Chapter Twenty-Eight

Luke awoke with the mother of all headaches, opening his eyes and closing them quickly as his head pounded and stomach rippled.

Somehow he'd landed on the floor, his cheek pressed to the carpet, one arm curled under him, dead, the other splayed out. With effort, he rolled onto his side and took another moment to push into a sitting position. The room tilted and he pressed the heel of his hand against his head, startled when it came away wet. He stared at the dark splotches in confusion.

Memory twisted with pain, and horror had him lurching to his feet, only to drop to his knees when his body dissolved beneath him. Blinking hard, his gaze fell on the heavy flashlight lying a few feet away. Sickness crept up the sides of his belly and beads of sweat rolled into his eyes. Trying again, he managed to push up onto the bed before struggling to stand again.

"Rowan!" he roared, wincing when the sound bounced inside his throbbing skull. He tried not to retch.

Pulling on his jeans, he used furniture to brace himself, stumbling through the open apartment door. He dimly noted Josephine's scent before grabbing the banister to work his way downstairs without tumbling and breaking his neck.

He screamed her name again, quickly blinking away the spread of darkness behind his eyes. Glancing to the right, he saw the barricade by the backdoor and staggered ahead, stopping and almost falling just before the pile of furniture by the front.

Breathing hard, he contemplated a few moments before returning the way he'd come and careening through into the kitchen. A cool night breeze fluttered against his face from the broken window. He stared at the small opening, not doubting she'd been able to wriggle through, but certain it had been an uncomfortable, probably painful, squeeze.

Heart thrashing, he worked his way past the kitchen to the bar to grab the landline. For the longest moment, he stared at it, unable to remember the number he needed, before it occurred to him to check numbers dialed. With an unsteady hand, he pressed what he needed, concentrating on the steady ringing, praying David would pick up, praying it wasn't too late for Rowan.

"This better be good, 'cuz I'm not on duty for another four hours," the man mumbled, voice thick with sleep and annoyance.

"Dave, it's me." Luke kept his hand pressed to his head in a possibly futile attempt to keep it from falling off.

His friend's tone changed in an instant. "What happened?"

"I don't think your mother's protection spells worked."

Dave remained silent at the other end for one long moment before repeating his initial question. "Luke, what happened?"

"Um…" He paused, remembering the large flashlight on the upstairs carpet. "I don't think Rowan would normally hit me with a blunt instrument and take off. I know I tend to piss her off at times, but whacking me one still seems out of character." His voice slid into a tunnel and he made another conscious effort to pull his murky brain together.

"Shit. You need an ambulance?"

"No, I just need to find her." He expected he had a concussion but didn't give a flying fuck. Despite the spinning of his head, fear for her made it and everything else insignificant.

"Okay, we're on our way."

Luke disconnected and worked his way to the front, intending to remove the barricade. Dully, he watched chairs and tables slide away.

"Thanks, guys," he heard himself mutter from a distance before the room tilted to knock him off his feet again.

****

Luke opened his eyes to the sound of the front door opening. He hadn't been able to unlock the door and it took him a blurry moment to remember he wasn't ever alone in the old building. At least not really.

Confused, he rolled onto his side, looking up to see Ruth and David Leroux stepping across the threshold. For the first time in memory, the woman looked old.

"Dear God!"

David crouched beside him, curling his hand around Luke's bare shoulder.

Any other time he would be self-conscious without a shirt, but he threw it aside before the discomfort could even hook into his brain. "I'm okay."

The man frowned, dubious. His gaze flicked back and forth between Luke's eyes, apparently looking for abnormalities. "You should get checked."

"No, I have to find Rowan." He sat up, waited for the swooping in his head to pass, and got to his feet with Dave's help, stopping to stare at the woman.

Face ashen, Ruth turned the way they'd come and kneeled down to remove the rubber mat and sweep the thick line of salt away from the front door. "Go. We'll follow you."

"Mama?" Dave frowned down at her, disquiet creased deeply into his features. "What are you doing?"

"He knows. He's going to her."

"Who knows?" Luke angled his head, frowning.

"Jimmy … Timothy." She gasped, the sudden chill around them bringing it out in a huff of vapor. She whispered, face slack in shock. "Both of you?"

"What?" Luke glanced at David, brain still muddled and unfocused. Anger and frustration layered onto his cold fear.

"She's not talking to us, man." He turned to study his mother, expression watchful, expectant.

Ruth stiffened and shuddered and when she pivoted to face them, her eyes and expression had gone blank. Her words, however, weren't. "C'mon, you two. David, help that boy. We have to go now." She walked out the door, spine yardstick straight.

"Shit." David stared and pressed his palm to his forehead.

"There's something wrong with her." Luke wavered and his friend slid forward to steady him before pulling him along.

"Yeah, there is. Mama's housing one of your spirits."

****

They'd left the freeway miles back, now twisting and turning on back roads barely wider than the old SUV. Headlamps lit their direction, while the three-quarter moon above dusted thick and knobby, bald cypress trees in an eerie, pale glow.

Rowan tried to keep track of every turn, but each one had little marker she could distinguish. As a city girl, her directions consisted of buildings and landmarks, not trees, brush, wetlands, and wildlife. Lost and turned around, she decided to instead concentrate on residential lights.

But those had become few and far between as the

SUV tires continued to bump and shimmy along the uneven road.

With effort, she isolated and flexed every muscle she could. They didn't like it, protesting with jabbing pins, but persistence made them acquiesce to her. Rowan could only hope they'd be strong enough. She'd come to the obvious conclusion that she would have to save her own ass. There'd be no Calvary riding in to the save the day. She was on her own.

"We are almost there." The man flashed a huge smile at her. "It's not much, but I find it comfortable and of course the swamp has its own beauty. In the morning or evenings, I can step out on my deck and see any number of wild creatures. Of course, sometimes they might wind up on the menu, but mostly I like to watch them lumber along, doing what they're doing. They have a very simple mindset. Survive and procreate. Humans are no different. Oh, we like to pretend we are, with our technology, fancy clothes, and cars, but when it comes down to the baser instincts, we're just animals."

He reached over to pat her leg and she winced in recoil and disgust.

Ady went on as if having a pleasant two-sided conversation. If he noticed anything from her, he gave no indication. "No, girl, we all fight to live and breed. I never had children myself, though. My wife and I couldn't. I buried her years before you were even born. I suppose I could have tried again, but I'm a one-woman man. There's just no one else I could ever want."

What was the purpose of even going on if there was nothing to look forward to? Was it habit, or fear of the unknown? She found herself trying to form the words but let them die in her throat. Horrified to feel a thread of sympathy, Rowan batted it away to work on her muscles, work on her breathing, and calm her heartrate.

Compassion or not, she knew she'd soon have to fight.

He turned one more time, guiding the SUV toward a house little more than a shack. It rose on stilts, backing against thick foliage. When he cut the engine, the thick musk and earthy smell of swamp pressed in from around them. "All right, this is it. Quite isolated, I know, but I like it that way. From here, most directions will bring you eyeball to eyeball with gators, water moccasins, even black bears. Every year we hear about some tourist losing themselves, dying in all kinds of unfortunate ways. It's never pretty."

Ady climbed out and came around to open the passenger door. Leaning in, he touched her face and smiled. "Huh. I can see you in there. I have to say I'm quite impressed. Most people are urinating themselves at this point, but not you. You're scared, I know, but my, what a temper! It's keeping you from turning into a little puddle of terror." He laughed. "Listen to me. I'm suddenly quite the poet."

Her respiration stayed fast and shallow, perspiration gleaming against her fair skin. Her eyes rolled toward him, away, and back. He tilted his head, studying her, mood sobering. "You may not believe this. Of course you wouldn't. But I am sorry. You shouldn't have to pay for the sins of your family, but unfortunately for you, if it's between your life and mine, I'm going to choose mine. It always goes back to that survival instinct I mentioned."

A solitary tear tracked down her face and he gently brushed it away with his thumb. "None of that, child. You were doing so well. You have to trust me. Once you go under, I promise you won't feel a thing. Now, come with me. I have preparations to make."

****

He took her arm and pulled her from the SUV

and toward the little house. Ady guided her up the back stairs, noting the movements of her body. They were still wooden, jerky, but less so.

The drug in her system would wear off shortly, so she would need to be subdued while he prepared for the ceremony. But that was okay. She didn't worry him. Soon he'd be back to his old self. He smiled in anticipation. He'd shed this horrible weakness like a snake discards its old skin.

And afterward, like all the others, he'd let the gators have her.

Chapter Twenty-Nine

The house wasn't any more inviting on the inside than it was on the outside. A cheap, fiberboard coffee table and end tables perched before and next to a worn floral sofa, while a card table and folding chairs filled the small dining room. Blank walls reflected scuffed plank floors with no area rugs. Rowan didn't even see a television or stereo. It wasn't a home, only a place to step in out of the rain, as far as she could tell. She would have found it depressing at any other time.

The smell of mildew and the faint acrid aroma of smoke burned her nostrils. Just beneath, permeating the room and everything within, was the dusty aroma of decay.

"I have a few preparations to make, but I promise it won't be long. I'll make sure you're comfortable while you wait though." Ady kept his hand at the small of her back. In Rowan's mind's eye, she could picture snapping every digit resting against her. "You'll need to be subdued naturally. I apologize for that, but I'm sure if you put yourself in my place, you'd understand."

Rowan swallowed her fear and poked at her temper to build it into a flare. There wasn't any more time. Her body was almost her own and the element of surprise was always a powerful attack. Ruth had thought him weak, and the thin, skeletal figure beside her seemed to prove the assumption. She only hoped it would be enough.

Wheeling around, she put all her weight into a roundhouse punch, keeping her thumb on the outside to reduce the chances of hurting herself. His head jerked back and blood erupted from his nose. In a frenzy, Rowan lashed out again and caught him across the ear.

Shock glazed his face, but when she went for his nose again, he blocked the assault. She managed to catch him with her other hand, raking her nails down his cheek. A growl rumbled from her throat, purified rage circling around and pressing in. Homicidal thoughts erupted from her primal brain. She wanted to hurt him badly, wanted to even kill him if the possibility arose. She kicked him in the shin hard enough to make her toes ache inside her sneaker and immediately swung out with another punch. Snarling, he bared his teeth and made a grab for her arms, but Rowan took advantage of the sudden proximity and kneed him in the groin. The man's already pale face lost any hint of color and he crumpled.

Giddiness with a hysterical edge soared through her. The fight part was over. It was time for flight. She wasn't sure where, but her instincts blared that it was time to go. She whirled to run, but he lurched forward and whipped out a hand to grab her ankle. His fingers bit in like teeth and he yanked her off her feet. Pitching forward, she reached out to break the fall, the brunt of her right hand taking her weight. Pain shot up from wrist to her shoulder, hot and bright as small bones snapped. She cried out, kicking at him as he flipped her onto her back, climbing up over her like a huge gangly spider. Blood dripped from his nose and filled the scratches under his eye, but he bared his teeth in a humorless grin.

When he reared back, she expected a blow. Rowan tried to scramble away, faltering with a whimper when her broken wrist refused to support her. Instead of hitting her, he billowed his cheeks and blew a fine white powder into her face.

She pulled in a quick breath in panic, coughing as the dust burned her sinuses and the inside of her throat. Jerking her head to the side, she gasped for fresh air, but a warm haze began to spread over her brain, numbing her from the inside out. Her tense muscles liquefied and she blinked up at him, anger ebbing into a fine mist.

"That, little one, is enough of that." Climbing to his feet, he shook his head and perched his hands at his hips. He stared down at her, something perversely like disappointment smearing his bloodied features. Ady looked at her as if she were a child sneaking a cookie before dinner, not a woman fighting for her life. With a deep sigh, he reached down to grab her under the arms.

Rowan rolled her bleary gaze around the little house, dull, but curious, as he dragged her down the short hall, past one doorway, but into another at the end. She was aware of the pain in her wrist, but it seemed disconnected and far away.

He gently laid her out in the center of a small room, arms and legs splayed out like a discarded doll's, heavy and useless. There was only one window centered on the north wall, hidden from the outside by blackout drapes. A large bookcase filled with all manner of jars and books stood opposite the door. Rowan tilted her head back to view it upside down, trying to focus on reading the spines, giving up when everything kept blurring.

Sleep would be good. She'd feel so much better after a nap. Her lids sagged, but a moment later, flipped them back open. The spark of fear and anger buried deep kept trying to scratch to the surface, and she wanted to concentrate on it.

But she was so tired.

Rowan wondered what Luke was doing and tried to clear away the murky lines from his image. Did he even realize how handsome he was? She could stare at him all day if she could get away with it. He had the cutest dimples when he smiled.

Memory cut a jagged hole through her and she couldn't stifle the sob.

She'd killed him.

No, she couldn't have. One part of her mind clung to that small sliver of hope, while the other embraced the certainty of his death.

Rowan wanted to scream, but little to no strength allowed only a weak cry. Hot tears slid from the corners of her eyes and ran down to dribble onto the hard floor.

"You've left me no choice but to begin a little early. But that's okay. I can take care of a few things afterward." There was no rancor in his voice, just acceptance.

Ady slid in and out of her vision, his movements accompanied by the clinking of glass and the pop of broken seals. She had no idea what he was doing and no longer had the presence of mind to endeavor to figure it out.

The dark room came alive with the flicker of candles. Shadows and flames came together to form frenetic pictures over the walls and ceiling. Smoke stung her eyes and the pungent aroma from some kind of incense or herb burned from around her.

His fingers touched her face, drawing and swirling shapes with a warm liquid. A metallic smell bit into the smoke around her and she wanted to ask him what he was doing. Couldn't do much but roll her head away from him.

Grabbing her face with one big hand, he completed the last stroke. Pausing, he stared down at her and his eyes widened. A startled and grateful smile twisted his thin lips. He pulled up her sweatshirt, drawing on her lower belly. "I'm sorry."

"Get off…" She tried to raise her voice to demand that he get the hell away from her, but the words stuck, gummy and thick in her throat. Rowan willed her fists to clench and lash out, but the best she could do was twitch her fingers. Something in his smile had her terror racketing up even higher, but there was no fight left now. She let her lids drop, wondering what death would bring. He'd said she wouldn't feel anything. Her thoughts and body felt detached from one another and she slowly realized he hadn't lied. She wouldn't feel pain when she died. She suspected the pain and suffering might come afterward in this man's warped world.

Words rumbled above her in an unfamiliar tongue. They blended together into a low hiss as they came faster, chanting.

Trying again, she struggled to part eyelids that must have weighed fifty pounds each. His face was wild with contortions as if small snakes struggled to burst free from his flesh. Those intense green eyes had rolled back in his skull, but the words continued, white noise unrecognizable to her.

It was like looking through a funhouse mirror, all distortion, all unreality. Smoke hung in the air above her, twisting and pulsing in a rhythm synonymous with the man's chanting. Her mind slid away, but she pulled it back with tenuous will, knowing in her gut that she wouldn't be able to fight much longer.

Acceptance began to weave its way inside. She'd lost. It was almost over.

When the man stumbled back with a cry, she frowned and calmly observed through tunneled vision. Bewilderment and curiosity settled over her, but it felt distant, as if she were watching everything from the nosebleed section of a large amphitheater.

Smoke thickened in the room, sliding and shifting around the man. He danced in bone jerks and flapping arms. His mouth moved, gaping and snarling. High-pitched screams loosed from his throat. She'd never heard such a sound from a male before.

No, not dancing. Fighting. There was someone else, another figure hiding in the smoke. They grappled in a peculiar ballet, Marcus Ady seeking escape, the other pursuing. She couldn't tell who her savior was. There was no face, just the impression of body and motion.

Rowan pulled a deep breath in, coughing out the polluted air, only to suck it in again. Dark splashes blocked her narrowed vision when her lungs grew too heavy. Exhaustion succeeded in falling over her, a thick, wet blanket at once stifling and oddly comforting. It pressed down, compressing her chest, her mind, her body.

At the sound of smashing glass, she let go.

Chapter Thirty

It wafted in the air, just the barest scent of smoke caught within the breeze.

"You need to hurry." Luke leaned forward from the backseat, eyes fixed through the front window as dawn broke around them. The tension in his body locked his muscles, while his head and neck throbbed in pain. He ignored the discomfort even as his heart rammed into his ribs in horror and agitation.

"If we bottom out, we won't be going anywhere." David snapped.

Ruth sat straight in the passenger's seat, saying nothing other than offered directions. Whichever spirit shared the woman's body was either subdued or biding its time. Luke would have bet on the latter.

"Turn here."

Dave glanced over at his mother, nodding.

The glow before them was unmistakable. Luke felt like an anvil had been dropped in his gut. Grabbing for the door handle, he tumbled out before the car had come to a complete stop. Somewhere on the other side of his panic, he heard David's demand to wait, but ignored it.

A man burst through the second-floor window in a spray of glass, landing several feet from the chicken coop in a tangle of smoke tendrils and frenzied movement. Two indistinct shadows twisted around him as inhuman screaming pulsed through the night air, quelling natural sounds from the swamp.

Without sparing the writhing figure in the yard more than a glance, Luke bounded up the stairs, pushing through the front door in a low crouch. Falling back a few steps, he pulled his borrowed jacket up to press against his nose and stumbled into the dense smoke. Narrowing his eyes, he swept the front rooms. Finding no one, he headed down the hallway, choking from lack of oxygen.

The first room held nothing but a cot and small bureau.

He moved on to the second, flinching at the fire engulfing the heavy drapes in the room. A mild breeze from the broken window fanned the inferno, whipping it into a frenzy and propelling it upward through the ceiling. A small, prone figure lay in the middle of some kind of intricately drawn symbol on the floor. One outstretched arm rested less than a foot from a tipped candle and the trail of flames.

His lungs burning and kicking, he coughed violently even as he leaned down to swoop her up. Blinking back the dots in his line of sight, Luke tossed Rowan over his shoulder and bulled his way out.

Sweet air chased out the soot and smoke as he made his way back down the stairs, carrying her far enough to keep safe from the spreading fire. A violent tremor bubbled from within and Luke coughed until his eyes watered.

Lying the woman down in the yard, a second spasm of coughing bent him forward a second time, hacking out ash and rancid air. When he could see again, he checked her pulse and leaned down to detect her breath.

"Jesus, Jesus, Jesus…" He was barely aware of the mantra slipping between his lips. Gently, he pushed tangled hair back from the damp skin of her face. He noted the bruising and swelling of her wrist absently and discarded it as superficial. But her face. No, no. Please. Dead white under soot and painted blood, except for a mouth tinged with blue. Her eyes were thin slits, unseeing. Cold sweat beaded on his upper lip, profound terror stealing in, blackened and ancient.

"No, no, no, baby. Don't do this to me!" He covered her mouth with his to push oxygen into her lungs, before beginning CPR. His mind went blank, concentrating on the task, not allowing himself to think beyond. The rhythm was second nature to him and he slipped into his zone.

He became conscious of someone resting a gentle hand on his shoulder, but he shook it off, determined to complete his task. He had to save her. He couldn't fail. No, not again.

"Come on, Rowan. Open those eyes. Come back and look at me." The words leaked from between clenched teeth, sweat dripping from his chin. "Fucking open them. I'm not kidding."

Thirty compression, two breaths, repeat, repeat…

"Luke." David's low voice reached down to him, ripping into his heart with its sympathy.

"Don't touch me." He didn't recognize his own growl or the despair within. Get into the zone. Compressions, breathe for her, keep it going… "He didn't kill her. We made it in time."

Somewhere in the distance, he thought he heard the wail of a sirens. He was certain of it a second later.

"Hang in there, baby. Just a little bit longer. You know something, Rowan O'Herley? I'm in love with you, so don't you dare fucking die on me."

The bokor's screams abruptly cut away somewhere beyond them, but Luke was barely conscious of it and he continued CPR. Everything constricted around him and sweat ran in his eyes. He impatiently wiped them against his shoulder and continued his rhythm.

"Come on back. You're tough. I know you can do

it."

Her sudden scalding breath, followed by another and a long fit of agonized coughing, had a hysterical laugh breaking through his own raw throat. He stroked her hair, leaned in to brush a kiss to her lips. "There you go, there you go…"

"Luke," Rowan whispered, staring up at him, eyes glazed and unfocused.

"Hey gorgeous." Overwhelmed and shaking, he traced his fingers down her filthy face.

"Thank God!" Ruth dropped beside them, wriggling out of her sweater and laying it over the young woman. Her face was pinched, dark eyes blazing in worry. "David called this in. All of it."

Rowan's body jolted and she tried to sit up, terror widening her eyes within her soot-covered face. "Where … is he?" A harsh new coughing fit brought her back down and Luke cradled her against him. Her eyes closed and he pressed his lips to the top of her head.

"Dead." Ruth met Luke's eyes, her voice shaking. "The spirit guiding me joined the other one as soon as you left the car."

Reading into her meaning, he took a breath and glanced behind him.

Several yards away, the man's body lay within tufts of thick weeds. The tall grass obscured most of the corpse, but he was fairly certain the man's face and throat had been torn into bloody ribbons.

"Jimmy guided us here. But that boy, Timothy … he got here first and ripped that man apart from the inside out." She sucked in a quivering breath. "So much rage."

"Timothy. The quiet one. The one I didn't know was at the tavern."

Ruth squeezed her eyes shut for a moment and nodded. "That boy was trapped inside one of Marcus

Ady's talismans. When Jimmy destroyed those vessels, Timothy was released and attached himself to Jimmy. I think he was forced to watch as Ady mentally broke the man."

"So, when he saw the same thing happening to Rowan, by the same hand…"

"Possibly, but I think he may have reacted more to Jimmy's distress. And his own memories of death and subsequent imprisonment."

"Jesus." Luke crinkled his brow. "Not to be unappreciative or anything, but why the hell did they wait until now to kill the guy?"

Ruth sighed, fatigue adding a few years to a face normally unlined. "I think the spell being cast tonight was as dangerous to Ady as it was to Rowan. If he'd been allowed to finish, well, you know what the result would have been. But there may have been a small window of vulnerability. That's what Timothy, and then, Jimmy, found."

Beyond them, firefighters spread out to gain control of the blaze. Luke expected the twisted little house would soon be charred and skeletal. He hoped the swamp would take it into its rancid depths. Let the gators and snakes have it.

David fell into a crouch next to them, relief evident when his gaze found Rowan listless but at least breathing. The EMTs were just behind him, lugging equipment and rolling a gurney. "Jesus, I thought she was gone. I'm glad I was wrong, man."

Luke buried his nose in Rowan's hair, despite the stink of smoke, and listened to her raspy but steady breathing. "So am I."

Chapter Thirty-One

Rowan sat up in bed, curled forward and hugging her knees.

She'd spent the last two days in the hospital and now waited, tension freezing her muscles, for formal discharge.

Her memories of that night were a blur of movement, darkness, and flames. When she worked at pulling out something solid, it resulted in a major banger of a headache. It didn't keep her from trying though.

A cast to her elbow encased her wrist, she'd been treated for smoke inhalation, and her system flushed of whatever substance Ady had used on her. Because some of it was unfamiliar to the medical world, they kept her an extra day to be certain there'd be no side effects. Now, she'd been deemed ready to go home.

But then there was still the other thing. An unexpected and troubling twist on an already unbelievable situation.

She rocked, wincing in pain from her wrist and a thousand additional sore spots but didn't stop. Her mind twirled, dipped, and frequently lost focus. Trying to rein it back, she gazed out the window, the view of the blue sky and puffy clouds partially blocked by another wing of the hospital.

A volunteer armed with a wheelchair, tight, curled gray hair, and an endearing smile shoved into the room. "Looks like your discharge papers are all in order and you're ready to go. Do you have someone picking you up?"

Rowan nodded, numb. "He's pulling the car around."

Luke had borrowed Andy's sedan and was

probably already waiting for her at the front entrance at that very moment. Facing him scared the crap out of her.

"Okay then. Hop in."

Rowan settled into the wheelchair while the volunteer adjusted the foot rests. Her mind drifted again, worry deep seated and holding.

It shouldn't have to be like this. She'd survived her experience, Marcus Ady was dead, and she no longer had to live with his darkness hanging over her. She had a successful business, friends, a city she'd grown to enjoy, and a man she loved.

She just didn't know how he felt about her, not exactly. It was obvious he cared, but she couldn't know to what extent. Luke was a complicated person, damaged from life and loss, and she couldn't even come close to predicting his reaction.

Shit. She couldn't even come to terms with it herself.

"Here. You hold these on your lap. It would be a shame to forget them." The volunteer handed her the vase filled with irises, lavender, and roses, a large teddy bear and a basket with fruit. The first had been sent by Ruth and David. Rowan managed a small smile. She owed them her life. The bear was a sweet acknowledgement from her staff at The Goose and the fruit had come from an astonished Margie. Rowan awkwardly juggled to keep them all from sliding to the floor.

The old woman pushed her through the corridors, down to the ground floor, and out through the front entrance, chatting the whole time. Rowan caught pieces of current events, seven grandchildren, three Chihuahuas, one twenty-year-old cat, and a parrot that swore in Portuguese.

Luke leaned against Andy's sedan, hands folded

across his broad chest. A gentle breeze ruffled his short, dark hair. Sunglasses blocked his midnight-blue eyes. He grinned when the volunteer wheeled her forward, and Rowan's stomach clenched.

Taking her gifts, he wedged them all into the backseat, before leaning over to help her into the car. He hesitated when she gasped in discomfort.

"I'm fine, Luke." She smiled up at him, hoping it didn't look too phony.

Nodding, he jogged around the car to slide into the driver's side, pulling away when they were clear. He guided the car through downtown traffic, glancing over at her every so often. His nervous energy was unusual and it ramped up her own.

"You must be starving. I thought we'd stop for muffulettas. Unless you have a craving for something different."

At her quick anxious look, he frowned. "Are you angry with me for some reason? I'm trying to think what I might have done, at least recently, but I'm drawing a blank."

"No, I'm not angry. Sharing a muffuletta with you would be great."

"Okay then." He shot another wary glance at her and she sighed. She'd have to come clean and let the pieces fall as they may.

Parking was always a challenge in the French Quarter, but he managed to locate a spot across the street from the restaurant. Waiting until a horse and carriage plodded by, he parallel parked with little effort before reaching for the door handle. The gentle pressure of her hand on his arm stopped him and he turned to study her. His expression slid into the careful blankness she hated.

Rowan pulled in a breath and let it out slowly to calm the thrashing of her heart. When it didn't work, she

tried again. "Um, there's something you should know …
and to be honest, I'm not sure how to go about it."

"Are you going to tell me to take a hike?"

Startled, she shook her head. "No, no." A nervous
and humorless chuckle shook her. "But you might."

"I'm going to tell me to take a hike?"

"Please stop. You're not helping." She pressed
the heel of her hand to her forehead. Everything trembled
inside and out. Even her skin seemed to shake. "Okay,
I'll just say it. Like pulling off a Band-Aid, right? That
would be best."

"Okay." He smiled in memory.

"Luke, I don't know how it happened. Wait, well,
I do know, but it shouldn't have happened." She looked
up at him and the words tumbled out in a rapid-fire
torrent. "I'm pregnant."

They stared at one another, her stinging,
brimming eyes meeting his calm blue ones. A sob caught
in her throat and she swallowed it down.

After several long moments, he tilted his head,
his big hand reaching for and enfolding her much smaller
one. "Do you love me, Rowan?"

Unsure how to read his response, she debated
before deciding to lay it all out with a tiny truthful nod.
"Yes."

"That's good. I'm glad." His thumb stroked the
back of her hand. "Because I love you wildly. More than
I ever thought I could. I honestly didn't think I could
ever feel this way again. I thought I had the one shot and
that was it. But I now know that's not true. I have a
second chance and I don't plan on blowing it."

She stared at him, her mind not quite grasping his
reaction and words. She'd set herself up for annoyance,
irritation, maybe even fury, but he watched her with such
a tender glow that her heart shimmered in her chest.

Rowan opened her mouth, closed it, and opened it. "I thought you'd be upset."

"You thought wrong." Luke gazed at her with warmth and amusement before it faded ever so slightly. "That moment I thought I lost you was one of the worst in my life. I'm so damned thankful I didn't. As far as I'm concerned, this pregnancy is a beautiful bonus."

"You don't seem surprised."

Luke raised and dropped a shoulder. "I suspected when you ate more than I did the other night. To be honest, the prospect freaked me out a bit. But then I saw what he did…" His eyes flashed for a moment before he brought his dark fury under control. "That freak show drew ceremonial symbols on your face, but also on your stomach."

All the moisture in her mouth evaporated. "The baby would have been a bonus soul for him. A pure energy. How the hell could he have known? I didn't even know."

"Some kind of spirit hotline, maybe? Ruth might know, but it doesn't really matter now, does it? What matters is we move on. Leave that bastard behind us. Let him feed the worms." Luke smiled. "We should go eat, but there was something else I wanted to bring up."

His smile ebbed a little in discomfort. "And I know that was a weird little bit of juxtaposition there. Sorry."

Her brain reeled free and out of control. Her announcement hadn't fazed him. It was the complete antithesis to what she'd expected. With effort, she focused back on his face, the clear brow, his straight nose, the strong jaw coated with two days of stubble, the dimples when he smiled, and those amazing eyes. He was beautiful. She doubted he even knew it. "What did you want to bring up?"

"It's a little something to piss off your mother."

She frowned, confused. "Well, that doesn't take much."

With an audible sigh, he reached into his pocket. "I was going to wait until we were chowing down on a sandwich bigger than your head, but now actually seems better. If it's not the right time, I'm sure I'll be able to read it all over you."

He pulled out a small felt-covered jewelry box and flipped it open.

Rowan didn't breathe, could only stare stupidly. "Is that...?"

"Yeah, it is. I'd like you to marry me, give the kid a name, and all that. Not that a modern woman really needs it, but ... well..." He stopped, frowned, and started again. "Look, I love you. I want you to share your life with me. If you would."

She let her gaze meet his and drop to the solitaire diamond, before roaming up to meet his again. When her heart thrummed and her words stuck, Rowan cleared her throat. Tears pressed from under her lids and one got away before she could stop it. She could barely believe this was happening, but her words were pristine and true. "I love you, Luke, and would love to marry you. Even if it does piss off my mom."

Her surly bartender beamed, threaded the ring onto her finger, and pulled her into a kiss that steamed the windows and prompted most passersby to smirk or grin.

Epilogue

The private courtyard was alive with the sounds of chatter and laughter. Friends and staff milled around, nibbling snacks, drinking, and laughing. Luke wove his way through the small crowd, stopping to smile, nod, and accept and exchange pleasantries. He figured the fake grin plastered on his face didn't fool anyone, but they knew him well and were polite enough to let it pass.

Henry sat on a side bench, his cane hanging on the armrest next to him. Margie sat beside him and they both smiled up at Andy as he rambled at them. It had taken a while for the old man to come back, and while he'd never be one-hundred percent, he was close enough to enjoy his family, pilgrimages to The Goose, and painting. He looked past his son and nodded to Luke, who returned the gesture.

Seeking escape and the important things, he pushed open the back slider to step into the cool dining room. The condo wasn't huge, but it fit their personalities with the charm of old brick, crown molding, two transoms, original wooden floors, and a high sweeping ceiling. As a fixer upper, they'd even managed to snag it at a deal, considering the cost of real estate in the French Quarter. He'd spent six months sanding, staining, painting, and swapping out fixtures. As a bonus, it stood three short blocks from the tavern.

Luke strode down the short hallway, photos old and new. From just ahead, he caught the low, sultry voice of his wife humming "Blackbird."

He stopped at the first bedroom on the left and leaned against the doorjamb to rest his gaze on the woman and child. Nightmares had plagued him for months after Rowan's near miss. Although they'd lessened, he still sometimes worried his second chance would disappear. He feared he would wake up back in that storage room at The Galloping Goose. Then he'd open his eyes to find her sleeping soundly beside him, red hair spread over her pillowcase and across his shoulder. He wouldn't change it for anything.

"You're being creepy." Her voice reached to him, soft and teasing. As always, a loving glow centered in his chest, bringing peace and contentment.

He twisted his mouth into a smirk. "Hey."

Rowan looked up and tilted her head, a smile warming her face. "Sorry for deserting you. He was hungry."

"Well, a man's gotta eat when a man's gotta eat." Luke stepped inside the little room with walls covered in marauding jungle animals and dropped to a crouch beside the glider. He reached out to run a gentle hand over the baby's silken dark hair, still amazed by the boy's existence. At seven months, Jamie favored him in coloring and dimples but held fast to his mother's unusual pewter-gray eyes. The child made a contented sound deep in his throat as he nursed, one tiny hand resting against Rowan's soft flesh.

"Vous êtes un jeune homme miracle," he murmured, eyes affixed to his son.

Rowan touched Luke's face, trailing fingers across his jawline. "Vous l'êtes aussi."

"Working on your French?"

"Seems appropriate to assimilate with the locals. At least I'll know when they're talking smack about me." Her mouth twisted to the side in sarcasm, but the beautiful radiance of her face and eyes had his heart stammering.

"Damn, now I won't be able make fun of you." He chuckled but leaned in to kiss her. Her lips softened beneath his for a moment before he pulled back to gaze at her and the child in her arms.

"You're staring again." Rowan narrowed her eyes, but humor sparkled within.

"Mmm hmm." He wrapped one finger in her hair, kissed her again even as the baby cooed. "You're my other miracle."

The End

NANCY E. POLIN

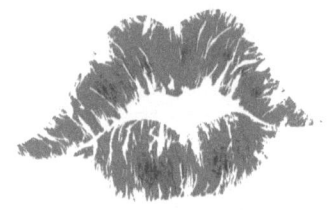

EVERNIGHT PUBLISHING ®

www.evernightpublishing.com

www.ingramcontent.com/pod-product-compliance
Lightning Source LLC
Chambersburg PA
CBHW030255200626
46816CB00002BA/653